WHERE *you belong*

A HEART'S COMPASS
BOOK FIVE

USA TODAY BESTSELLING AUTHOR
BROOKE O'BRIEN

WHERE YOU BELONG

A small town, single mom romance from USA Today Best-selling author Brooke O'Brien about a woman who returns to Arbor Creek to break free from her abusive marriage and learns to let love in again.

No one ever goes into marriage expecting it will end in divorce.

Every day became a struggle as I saw the man I once loved become someone I didn't recognize. But for my son, I knew I had to work up the courage to walk away.

Starting over in a small town wouldn't be easy, but it was close to my mom, and I needed her support. When the perfect home and a job all but fell in my lap, I couldn't help but feel like I was right where I was meant to be.

Corbin Reid walked into my life like he was meant to be there all along. His devilish smile and his smooth-talking ways are no match to the amazing heart he shows me. It didn't take long and I didn't stand a chance but to fall in love with him.

Our secrets always have a way of revealing themselves. When the truth comes out, the happiness I finally found comes crashing down around me.

Will our past tear us apart or will our love bring us right where we belong?

Thank you for reading **WHERE YOU BELONG**! I hope you love Corbin and Haelynn's story as much as I do.

You can join my Facebook group, Brooke O'Brien's Rebel Reader Group, to discuss the series and get sneak peeks on future releases. Sign up for my newsletter to find out more about my new releases. To join, visit: www.authorbrooke obrien.com/follow

Enjoy the story!

a heart's compass series
READING ORDER

WHERE I FOUND YOU

a small town, on the run, secret identify romantic suspense

LOST BEFORE YOU

a small town meets big city, friends to lovers romance

UNTIL I FOUND YOU

a small town, second chance romance

NOW THAT I FOUND YOU

an emotional and gripping surprise pregnancy, romantic suspense

WHERE YOU BELONG

a single parent, law enforcement, small town romance

Learn more and purchase your copy at:
www.authorbrookeobrien.com/heartscompass

prologue

HAELYNN

I've stared at the same text on my phone for the past thirty minutes. The dread filling the pit of my stomach is insurmountable. The darkness of the room nearly swallows me whole.

Sometimes I feel like I'm living two different lives.

During the day, I put on a brave face for my son. He's the only thing I have in my life to keep me going, and I fight every day to keep from burdening him with my pain.

When he drifts off to sleep, the sinking depression I've managed to keep at bay during the day threatens to break the barrier until nothing is left to fend it off.

I rub my fingers over my face. My hair falls around me like a curtain, and I continue my path, pushing them through the strands and gripping them in my fist.

Every night I sit here, overwhelmed by the impending moment when he'll come home, and I have nowhere left to run. Nowhere to hide.

Headlights flash through the window, and unease twists in my stomach like a knot. In the distance, I hear the faint sound of the garage door open, mixed with the steady beat of my heart hammering in my chest.

Tears fill the brim of my eyes, and my lips quiver as I fight to keep my emotions bottled up tight. I squeeze my eyes shut as a teardrop lands on my cheek and streaks down my face. I quickly swipe the palm of my hand over my damp skin and let out a heavy exhale.

It will get better. One day, it will get better.

I've repeated those words to myself so many times, I'm beginning to wonder if I believe them to be true or if I'm trying to will myself there.

The door leading from the garage into the house slams shut with force and jolts me from my thoughts. My hand pats around on the bathroom rug, searching for my phone to check the baby monitors to see if Huxton woke up from the noise.

Atlas is in one of his moods. I could sense it from the clipped responses in his text he sent me earlier tonight. As expected, he couldn't care less about the fact our son should be sleeping in the bedroom next to ours.

Huxton is fast asleep in bed with his little arm draped above his head. His soft snores are drowned out by the white noise machine. When enough time has passed without him moving or crying, I'm convinced the door slamming didn't wake him.

My husband is the reason I dread putting my son to bed. I know when I do, I'm only another minute away from when he'll walk through the door.

In the early part of our marriage, I spent so much time trying to convince him to come home earlier. I tried telling him how much I missed him, how hard it was doing it alone when he'd be gone anywhere from ten to twelve hours a day only to come home, eat, and go straight to bed.

In the beginning, he tried, but as the days went by, it started happening more and more until we were back to where we started. I've spent so much time crying, practically begging him to put us first.

I have no more energy left.

I can make out the faint sound of his footsteps coming up the stairs. I squeeze my eyes shut, wishing he'd change his clothes and go to sleep. I press the palms of my hands against my eyes, saying a prayer he'll leave me alone tonight.

When his footsteps draw near, I blink through the tears forming beneath the crack of the door. He doesn't bother knocking, reaching for the doorknob only to find it locked.

"You gonna lock me out of my own fucking bathroom?"

"I'm getting ready to take a bath," I lie.

It's not like it's a stretch, though. If it'll give me space from him, I'll do what I need to do. Sometimes I'll slip in here when he gets home, light some candles, and turn on soothing music to try to relax enough to fall asleep.

"Open the door." His stern voice sends chills up my spine.

I stand, hitting the light switch above the bathtub. It's soft, muted, and less harsh on my eyes. If he knew I was sitting here in the dark, he'd ask questions, and I don't think either of us is ready for the truth of my answers.

My eyes are red and bloodshot from crying. I do a quick swipe under my eye and try to shake the dread eating me up inside. I flip the lock and open the door as he pushes into the space.

His tall frame towers over me. He leans against the doorframe, his eyes roaming over my body, narrowing when they meet my face. The scent of alcohol on his breath wafts through the air.

It takes everything in me to fend off the urge to curl my lip in disgust at the thought of him driving home, further proving his selfishness.

"C'mere," he drawls, reaching his hand out toward me.

My body goes rigid. He rears his head back, staring down at me. The look on his face says it all. He can't believe I'd have the audacity to recoil from his touch.

"I said come here," he orders.

I take a step toward him, closing the distance between us. I force myself through the movements, pressing my hand against his chest. Despite our proximity, it doesn't escape my notice how distant we feel from one another.

He's no longer the man I married.

My heart doesn't race when he kisses me. My breath doesn't get caught in my throat when he touches me or looks at me from across the room. I don't even remember the last time we kissed or made love, let alone felt an ounce of passion behind it when we did.

My heart aches at the thought of living like this forever, of our son growing up and not seeing love between his parents.

"I'm fuckin' sick of you pulling away from me whenever I try to touch you. What kind of wife are you? Don't you understand I have needs?"

My eyes narrow, and unlike my restraint a moment ago, I don't attempt to shield my disgust. My lip curls, and I shake my head, but I'm not the least bit surprised.

"Why don't you ask yourself the same question, Atlas? What would make you think I'd want to be touched by you?"

His nostrils flare, and his face reddens with anger. His large hand pushes against my chest, and the force behind it sends my body crashing against the doorframe, causing me to cry out in agony.

"You need to remember who the fuck yer talkin' to, do you hear me? If yer not gonna let me fuck you, I'll have no problem findin' someone who will."

His words are jumbled together from the alcohol in his bloodstream.

He shoves his forearm against my chest, and my body collapses on the floor, recoiling from him and his touch. The look of revulsion on his face as he stands over me in a display of dominance lets me know it could've been much worse.

"Leave me alone," I spit out.

He clenches his jaw, shaking his head.

"Now, Atlas. I'm not fuckin' kidding anymore. I'm done! Leave. Me. Alone."

It's the first time I've ever uttered those words to him. The red-hot rage was apparent on his face.

"Who do you think you are turnin' me down? You'd be nothin' without me, you hear me? You'd have nothin'! If you try to leave me or take my son from me, I'll make your life hell. You understand?"

I never knew what hell was until I met him.

HAELYNN

ten months earlier

I guess I'd consider myself superstitious. You'll never find me walking under a ladder, crossing the path of a black cat, and if I see a penny on the ground, I will always stop to pick it up.

These days, I could use all the help I can get regarding a stroke of good luck.

I never expected at twenty-four years old I'd be packing up my life in a couple of hours while my husband was at work to take our son and move us to Arbor Creek.

I've spent the past four years married to a man who no longer resembled the one I fell in love with. People change as they grow older. We go through hard times, and each lesson learned makes us wiser.

Hell, if I'm being honest, I don't think I recognize the woman I see in the mirror either. I can't fault him for changing, but I blame him for the darkness he showed me as time passed.

I saw my opportunity to get out, and I ran like hell while I had the chance.

They say bad luck comes in threes. It started with finding out our dog had to be put down when a tumor in her spine ruptured to learning Atlas started the process of filing bankruptcy without ever telling me. The icing on the cake was finding out all those late nights at the office included stops by the strip club.

I was a stay-at-home mom to our son. Who knew that was the place where businessmen met up to talk about investments?

If the old wives' tale is true, I'm due for some good luck to show up.

After leaving Huxton with my mom this morning, I made the quiet drive across town to our new house and let myself soak in how right this moment had felt.

The first few weeks after we moved out weren't easy. We stayed with my mom for a couple of months, long enough to get back on my feet. I was eager for a place to call my own, though. With enough to cover our first month's rent and a little to fall back on, I took the leap.

If I didn't want to get in over my head, I needed to start looking for a job quickly.

Arbor Creek is a small town in Iowa. It's not far outside of Everton, which makes it the perfect place for me to raise Huxton, but it also makes it difficult to find a job. Securing employment is next on my list after I get settled.

A handful of boxes are left in the back of my mom's rusted old pickup truck. Sweat dots my brow from the summer sun blazing overhead. I lift the sleeve of my T-shirt and dab it across my forehead, exhaling a deep breath before hoisting another box into my arms.

My sneakers squeak against the hardwood floor leading down the hallway, and I drop the box on the island in the center of the kitchen. I dust my hands off and swipe the sweat off my face once more as the sound of glass shattering halts my movement.

"Oh no, no, no!" I wince, finding two of the four wine-glasses I just bought now broken on the floor. Of course, it happened right after I cleaned off the counters and swept the floor too.

My phone starts ringing as I'm sweeping the last of the broken shards into my dustpan. "Mom" flashes on the screen, and I swipe to answer the call.

"How are things going?"

"It's going well…" I trail off, resting my hip against the counter while staring at the two remaining glasses. "Or it was until a minute ago, when I accidentally broke some glass on the floor."

"What happened?" she asks, her voice growing con-cerned.

"I knocked a few glasses off the counter. It's not a big deal."

"Good." She sighed, causing my brows to furrow in con-fusion. "They say breaking glass in your new home is a sign of evil leaving your house, and good things are coming your way."

Something is oddly comforting about hearing those words right now.

"Well, I'll let you get back to work. When you're ready for us, let me know. We'll bring you some lunch."

We hung up after I told her I only had a few boxes left, and I was going to call it a day once I finished unpacking the kitchen. It wouldn't take long, considering we didn't have much. We didn't need much, though, either.

I knew when we left it wouldn't go over well with Atlas. He'd show remorse, tell me how sorry he was, and offer me the moon with all his meaningless promises. When that didn't work, he'd try to prove I was making a mistake and resort to begging.

I couldn't stand the thought of being stuck in an unhappy marriage for another day. If it took walking away from everything I owned and starting over, it was what I'd do. As long as I have Huxton, I have everything we need.

Everything else will come with time.

After hanging up with my mom, I put in another order at Target for pickup to get a replacement set of wineglasses. I would need those. Then I was back to work.

I hitch my leg up on the tailgate and climbed up into the bed of the truck, pushing the remaining boxes to the edge.

"Hey, neighbor," a friendly voice calls from behind me as I lift one of the boxes. I turn to see who it is, damn near tripping over my own feet. She jogs across the street toward me as I right myself again.

"Need a hand?" She laughs. She's taller, with long blond hair and a bright smile. She waves over her shoulder at the man behind her. The way he smiles at her is full of love, and she grins right back at him.

They are both dressed like they just got in a workout.

"I'm Madelyn." The girl smiles and extends her hand out to me. She points at the guy over her shoulder. "This is my boyfriend, Alex."

"It's nice to meet you," I say, dropping the box on the tailgate. "I'm Haelynn. I'll be living here with my son, Huxton."

Her smile softens at the mention of Huxton.

"I saw the 'For Rent' sign come down earlier this week and have been keeping an eye out for our new neighbors. It looks like you got most of it handled, but can we help with anything?"

"I would appreciate it." I smile. It's only a few more boxes, but the sooner I can wrap this up, the quicker I can finish unpacking the kitchen.

Alex sidesteps her and reaches for one of the boxes. Madelyn and I trail him, and I lead the way into the house. Madelyn follows me into my room with our two boxes while Alex deposits the one in Huxton's room.

"This is such a cute place," she gushes. "I've been looking forward to the day we welcome more people our age to the neighborhood. It's overrun with retired folks, which is great when raising a family in a quiet area, but like I said, it's so quiet."

"You only say that because you're still ticked at Mary Jean for calling Corbin when you were playing your music so loud."

She rolled her eyes. "It was the Fourth of July!"

Alex chuckled, squeezing her shoulder, and muttered, "I know, Penny girl. I know."

She smirked back at him and turned back toward me. "If you're not playing music, grilling out in your backyard, and lighting some sparklers, are you even American?"

I grinned, recalling all the memories of us doing the same growing up.

"She's got a point."

"You'll have to come over and hang with us sometime. Are you from the area originally?"

Over the years, I started to lose touch with the friends I had when I was younger. The thought of making new ones, especially so close by, has me thinking about what my mom said on the phone a little bit ago.

"My mom is from the area, but she moved out of town when she was pregnant with me. I was raised near Chicago but moved back to Everton a few years ago with my ex-husband to raise our son closer to family."

It is the first time I have spoken the word "ex" out loud to anyone since our separation. It feels strange rolling off my tongue.

She nodded, a look of sympathy passing over her face. "I'm from the area myself, but only moved in here with this guy a couple of months ago."

"It took a lot of cajoling, but I persuaded her to give me a chance. Once she did, she didn't want to let me go, so I convinced her to move in with me. I've got too much space for one person anyway." Alex chuckled.

"Yeah, it took a lot of persuasion." Madelyn smirks.

Something about the devilish smiles on their faces has me thinking they enjoyed whatever that entailed.

"I recently opened a photo studio in town, just down off Fallon Street. If you and Huxton would like family photos, I'll hook you up with a good deal."

My heart warmed at the thought of getting pictures taken with Huxton, just the two of us.

The mention of a photo studio in town spurred a thought after perusing job postings last night.

"Photo studio? You wouldn't happen to be talking about the one..." I pause, snapping my fingers in hopes it will help me remember the name of the place I bookmarked to my favorites. "Is it Memories and Moments?"

She smiles. "That's me!"

"I saw the posting online for an assistant. I was planning on applying this weekend."

"Are you kidding? What a small world." She smiles, her eyes lighting up. "I'll give you my number and when things settle down this weekend, shoot me a text message and we can chat more about the position. I'm looking to have someone start soon, so if you're interested, the sooner the better."

"That would be perfect. Huxton starts school next week, and I'm ready to get myself back out there."

She grins. "We can make that happen!"

Alex ducks out a few minutes later after assuring me he'll be around if I need a handyman. Madelyn stuck around after he left, chatting with me and lending a hand while we unpacked the kitchen.

She talked about how she and Alex met. He was from a small town in Wisconsin but met through mutual friends when he came to visit for a few weeks over the summer. They had spent every available second together, but when the time came for him to go back home, she wasn't ready to let him go.

Atlas and I did the long-distance thing for a while when he moved back to Everton and I was still in school. I know how hard it can be on a relationship, especially when you don't have your future all mapped out together.

Chatting with Madelyn brings back memories of my friends from Chicago. I made a mental note to reach out to them.

I can't shake how early this morning I had a good feeling things were around the corner. In a span of a couple of hours, not only did I make a new friend but I also had a job opportunity all but fall in my lap.

This is the start of the next chapter in my life, and for the first time in a long time, I'm excited about what the future has in store.

chapter two

HAELYNN

"All right, Huxie, you have fun with Gram, and I'll see you when I get off work."

He drops his toy truck on the floor from where he's standing in the middle of my mom's double-wide trailer and runs toward me, his arms flying around my waist, squeezing me in a hug.

This week has been big for the two of us.

"I love you, sweetie," I whisper, crouching down to wrap my arms around his small body. His dark hair and chocolate eyes reach into my chest and squeeze my heart.

Everything I do in life is for this boy, and I'd walk away from my marriage countless times if it meant keeping him safe.

"I love you too." His words are muffled from his small cheek pressed against the side of my arm.

He pulls back, lands a kiss against my cheek, and flashes me a huge grin before darting off to the living room.

The sound of my mom's heavy cough echoes down the hall. She strolls toward me, hair disheveled on one side and a large cup of coffee in her hand, evident she rolled out of bed not long ago.

"Quit worrying about the boy. He's with me, so he'll be fine. I did a decent enough job of raisin' you, didn't I? Now get outta here. Let me spend time with my grandson."

I exhale a chuckle and nod in agreement.

"I should be here just after four. I googled the address, and it's not too far from here."

"Of course it's not far. This is Arbor Creek. What did you expect? Now, go!"

I peer over at Huxton, but he's too busy lining up his toy cars to pay me any mind, so I sneak out the door, leaving them be.

Madelyn texted me last night to run through everything I'd need to know before my first day. We had talked off and on over the weekend. I couldn't believe how quickly we clicked.

The opportunity to work with her has come at the perfect time. I need a job as desperately as she desires an assistant. We covered more about what the position entailed. I'll be taking over scheduling appointments and running her social media, helping keep things running smoothly so she could focus her time and attention on all things photography.

She gushed over an idea she saw scrolling on TikTok and asked me if I'd help her with it. She didn't give me many details, just told me to bring some fall-inspired clothes and leave the rest up to her.

Although I have no idea what I am getting myself into, I know this is her baby, and she won't steer me wrong.

The GPS signals for me to turn right onto Fallon Street. A strip of businesses lines the main street leading into the small two-block downtown area. I spot Memories and Moments on the end and pull into the small parking area on the side street, leaving the space open in the front for customers passing by.

Iron lanterns hang against the dark brick building, giving off a cozy rustic vibe. The doorbell dings when I pull the door open, and the scent of coconut swirls through the air. The studio is open in the front, with a large desk in the center of the room separating the waiting area from the rest of the space.

There are candles lit along the counter, and soft music plays overhead. Something about the energy of the studio fits, and I feel right at home.

Madelyn peeks her head out of a doorway near the far back, her larger-than-life smile spreads across her face.

"Haelynn," she sings. "Oh my gosh, you're here!" She waves frantically, dashing toward me. "I'm so excited. Are you excited? I hope you are!"

Any hesitation or worry I may have been holding on to is gone when I see how happy she is. Her smile and personality are infectious.

"Very! It was hard to leave Huxton this morning, but we need this. I need this!" I press my palm to my chest, emphasizing how much I mean it.

She bounces on her feet, clapping her hands. Her eyes look from mine down to the bag in my hand.

"Oh good, you brought everything with you." She smiles, motioning for me to follow her.

There's a bed pushed against the wall, and a backdrop directly across from it with a wicker folding screen toward the back, likely where her clients go for wardrobe changes.

"Corbin should be here any minute. You'll love him. This will turn out perfect," she gushes.

My brows furrow as I'm pulling clothes out of my bag, laying them out to show Madelyn. I pause, wondering who the heck Corbin is?

"Does he work for you too?"

When we had spoken, she led me to believe she's been working here and running the studio by herself.

"No, he's a friend of mine. He's coming for the photo shoot." She motions her hand toward the clothes, seemingly confused by my question.

"Did you get the TikTok video I sent you last night?"

I shake my head.

"Oh, well, that makes sense." She chuckles. "It's for a stranger photo shoot. I got the idea from another photographer on TikTok. Here, let me show you."

She reaches for her phone in her back pocket. Pulling it out, she scrolls with her finger while my heart starts hammering in my chest.

She wants me to do a photo shoot with this… Corbin, and we've never even met.

I shake out my hands, trying to formulate the words to break this to her, but I don't think I'm the right person for the shoot. The guilt twisting in the pit of my stomach leaves me feeling uneasy.

This is my first day. I haven't even made it more than ten minutes, and I'm already disappointing Madelyn.

"Here it is." She grins, turning the phone toward me. It takes me a second to even focus on the screen. The video shows clips of two couples meeting for the first time and their various poses during the shoot.

You can see the connection between the two strangers even in the short video, and the anxious feeling of being able to give her the same makes my body tremble.

I shove the fears aside, though. Despite the worry of being unable to deliver, I'm an expert at covering up my emotions and putting on a brave face to prevent anyone around me from knowing how I feel.

"Wow, you can feel the connection between them. That's amazing!"

"Right?" Madelyn sighs, reaching for the phone to watch the video clip again before slipping it back into her pocket. "I thought it was a good idea to add to my collection of work and maybe entice some new clients to book their upcoming event with me. Anything will help, right?"

I didn't want to let her down by telling her how I haven't been touched by another man in over a year. Hell, it's been even longer since I was intimate with Atlas.

I'm not sure I can evoke the same emotions watching that clip, but I'll give my best effort.

She looks over the outfits I brought with me and assures me they'll be perfect.

"Oh, he's here!" she squeals. "You should get changed. Let me know when you're ready, and I'll walk you out, so we can start with the initial meeting. Does that sound good?"

I bite my lower lip, trying to stop the words on the tip of my tongue from slipping out. It's not that I don't want to do this or that I can't do this; it's more that I don't want to disappoint Madelyn.

She's been wonderful to me since we first met, and the last thing I want to do is to let her down.

I scoop the clothes in my arms and slip behind the divider to change.

"Oh, I left the mask to cover your eyes on the hook in the corner. Do you see it?"

"Yes," I croak out. "Yes, I do."

Standing in the mirror, I stare at the girl looking back at me. My mind flashes back to the nights I'd slip away to the bathroom, desperately seeking distance from him. I'd get lost in my mind staring at my reflection, thinking about how I ended up here and dreaming about the day when I'd break free. I was constantly walking on eggshells around him, and every second he was home began to feel like a countdown until the moment he would leave.

It dawns on me, taking in the look on my face, how different I look from the woman I saw a year ago.

The lost look I saw in my eyes doesn't look so distant, and the dark circles under my eyes have begun to fade away. My cheeks are fuller, and the sun-kissed tan highlighting my skin glows, reminding me of all the good things coming my way.

Something about seeing this change right now, on the brink of starting a new chapter in my life, has me letting out a heavy sigh of relief. It's the sign I needed, reminding me of how much change I've gone through and how many risks I've taken to get here.

The door dinging in the distance yanks me from my thoughts, pulling me right back into the present.

"Well, look who it is," Madelyn sings.

"Hey, darlin'." Something about his deep, raspy tone zips like lightning through my body, causing my stomach to flip.

I slip my shirt over my head, folding and setting it in a pile on the chair, leaving on the white tank top I'm wearing underneath.

"Thank you again for doing this for me."

"It's no problem. It's not like you had a lot of options. I can't imagine you wanting Alex to step in, and we both know it would take an act of God to convince Gage to do anything like this."

Madelyn laughs. "You're not lying."

I pull over the burgundy top, adjusting the cinched band around my waist. The sleeves are less fitted, flowing over my arms.

"I can't believe I let you convince me, though. Who wants pictures of me with a stranger?" He chuckles. "Although you did promise me she was beautiful, so how could I say no?"

Something about knowing he's nervous but was looking forward to meeting me is oddly comforting. I trust Madelyn, and although she doesn't know a lot about me or my past, I don't think she'd associate with a man she didn't trust.

I pull on my jeans, sitting snug on my hips, and step back into the booties I wore for my first day.

"How are you doing over there, Haelynn?"

A throat clears, and he mutters, "You coulda warned me she was listening."

I cover my mouth to contain my laughter.

"Give me just a second to get this mask on, and I'll be ready."

"You need to get your mask on too. Here," Madelyn says. "Now stand over here."

I picture her leading him to where she wants him.

The floorboards creak with footsteps walking toward me, and Madelyn's head peeks around the divider.

"Good choice! You look great," she whispers.

I shake out my hands, and she murmurs under her breath. "Don't be nervous. Corbin's one of the sweetest men I know, and you'll be great together. I promise!"

I rub my lips together, the gloss I put on earlier still coating them, pulling the mask over my face to cover my eyes. Madelyn slides her arm into mine, guiding me into the studio with her. The floorboards creak beneath us, and Andrew Jannakos plays through the speakers around us. I know when I get closer to Corbin, judging by the woodsy scent mixed with the clean smell of laundry detergent lingering in the air. It's a distinct smell that's all male.

Madelyn turns me to face the other direction and mutters for me not to move so she can grab her camera. I wring my hands out, rubbing them on the front of my jeans.

"Okay, I'm ready when you are."

I slip my mask off my face, blinking to adjust my eyes to the lighting, and glance over at Madelyn. She's ready and waiting, snapping pictures. The camera covers most of her face, but you can't miss her large grin as the camera clicks away.

I turn, and my eyes fall on Corbin, taking in the soft caramel of his eyes. Something about the sparkle mixed with the curve of his smile has me breaking out in a grin of my own.

"Goddamn, she wasn't lying. You are more than beautiful, you are… I don't even know the word."

His hands reach out toward me, pulling me into his arms. I toss my head back, a genuine laugh bubbling up from inside me, shaking my head.

"I'm not sure, but you sure know how to sweet-talk a woman, don't you?"

"Did it work?" He smirks. My hands glide over the tight ridges of his chest, my fingers gripping his shirt to pull him closer to me.

I forget Madelyn is in the room with us and drown out the sound of the shutter clicking with each picture she takes.

It's like everything around us falls away, and it's only the two of us. Any other time, I'd be second-guessing my every move, ruining the moment by analyzing every moment.

Not today. I'm rolling with it.

I'm seizing the day.

chapter three

CORBIN

Damn, Madelyn was holding out on me. Why didn't she tell me about her friend she hired at her studio sooner?

When Haelynn turned around, and I locked on those piercing brown eyes, I lost the ability to stream words together into a sentence.

When her soft hands found their way to my chest, I couldn't keep mine off her. I didn't hesitate to pull her into my arms as if we were about to slow dance, just the two of us.

Her skin was warm, and I couldn't help but wonder if it was both from her nerves and the initial attraction I felt pulling us together. It was a fine line, wanting to take it slow out of respect for her. I couldn't help but wish the cameras weren't here for the chance to get to know her more.

"Is this okay?" I whisper low enough for only her to hear.

She nods, peering down to where my hand is folded over hers, pressed against my chest before she slides it up around my neck.

"We'll go at your pace," I assure her. "I'm following your lead."

Her smile turns tense, and I worry she's pulling away from me. If I hadn't been paying attention to it, I would've missed it, but as quickly as it's there, it's gone.

"You guys are doing great," Madelyn assures us.

The song changes to one about spinning her around on the dance floor, and I reach for her hand.

"Dance with me," I murmur, and she grins.

I slip my fingers between hers, twirling her before pulling her back into my arms again.

With her back pressed against my chest, I skim my hand along her side, down to her hip. I dip my head down, pressing my cheek against hers. Her hair falls forward like a curtain, shielding her face from Madelyn.

"You fit so perfectly in my arms," I whisper.

She nods and her chest heaves, exhaling a heavy breath. Damn, what I wouldn't give to have her to myself right now.

I lace our fingers together, pulling her with me until my back is flush against the cool brick wall of the studio. Madelyn continues to murmur words of encouragement, but I don't pay her any mind.

I'm too lost in the moment with Haelynn. Just the two of us.

Haelynn gazes up at me beneath the long lashes fanning across her face with each slow blink. Her eyes are glossy with desire. I was thankful her back was to Madelyn because, damn, I wanted to reserve that look for only me.

"You don't know how hard it is not to kiss you right now."

Her eyes flash to my mouth as I drag my bottom lip between my teeth.

"Jesus," Madelyn mutters. "You can continue to pretend I'm not here, it's fine. I know you wish I wasn't, but I can't leave now. These photos are going to turn out fire."

The camera continues to click, snapping a series of pictures.

I trace my finger along Haelynn's jaw, tipping her mouth up until our lips are a hair's breadth away from touching.

I hesitate for a moment, wanting to give her the opportunity to pull back. I meant it when I said we were following her lead, but I'm still a man, so I won't shy away from letting her know what I want.

She tilts her chin up toward me in silent invitation. My heart hammers in my chest at the sight. Any second-guessing or worries she'd push me away are gone when I stare into her eyes. She darts her tongue out, slowly dragging it across her lips to wet them.

I growl under my breath, unable to hold myself back. I tilt my head down and press a soft kiss against her mouth.

She grins against my mouth while her fingers grip the front of my shirt, pulling me closer to her. She opens her mouth, her tongue dragging along my lower lip. I take the invitation and run with it, lacing my fingers with hers.

She releases a soft moan just before her tongue brushes mine.

How is this happening right now? I'll never know, but I'm too far gone at this moment and never want to come up for air.

I lean my forehead against hers when our lips finally break apart.

"What are you doing to me?" I whisper.

She pulls back, closing her eyes for a brief second. When her eyes finally meet mine, she flashes me an easy smile.

"You get your photos, Penny girl?"

"Yeah." Madelyn giggles. "I couldn't stop snapping them. I'll, uh, give you two a minute to yourselves."

I nod, not taking my eyes off Haelynn.

Madelyn's heels on the floor grow faint, signaling she's out of the studio, leaving me alone with Haelynn. She steps back, brushing her hand over her hair before tucking a strand behind her ear.

"You look perfect," I assure her.

She rubs her lips together, smothering her smile. "Thank you."

The way the words came out, genuine and sincere, made me almost want to ask when she was last told she was beautiful. I didn't, though, because I wasn't interested in bringing up the last person who told her, but she deserved to hear it every day.

"No thanks necessary, it's the truth."

"I heard Alex call Madelyn 'Penny' the other day. Is that some sort of nickname?"

"It's her call sign."

She nods, her eyes narrowing in confusion.

"Her dad, Maverick, is a former Army Night Stalker. He worked for Compass Security, which is how she and Alex met. He was visiting one of our friends, Gage, and helped with some work they were doing in the area. He started calling her Lucky Penny for good luck. I guess it sorta stuck with the rest of us."

"What do they call you?"

"Raven."

Her eyes widened, her brows shooting up in surprise. "What's that look for?" I asked.

"Raven?"

I nod. She turns, taking a few steps and sitting on the edge of the bed staged in the center of the studio.

"They say when a raven visits you, it's like a sign of a bad omen."

I chuckle, strolling toward her and having a seat next to her. "You believe in things like that?"

She shrugs. "Kinda."

"It also signifies recovery and healing. I guess it depends on how you choose to look at it."

Her eyes widen, and she nods, a hint of a smile peeking through.

"Madelyn mentioned you moved in across the street from her and Alex," I say, changing the subject.

"I did." She runs her palms over her pant legs, crossing her arms in her lap. I lean in, brushing my shoulder against hers, wanting to be close to her.

"I grew up not too far from there. My parents live just down the road, heading out of Arbor Creek. They built a big house on my grandparents' land before I was born, and they've lived there my whole life. It's right on the edge of town, along the highway, if you're heading in from Everton."

"Is that right?" I can sense her pulling away from me, her guard going up.

It's been so long since I've been in the dating scene. When you live in a small town, everyone knows everyone, meaning even casual dating can be hard.

I've been known to spend time with several women in town, but it was never serious. Now, here I am sitting with Haelynn, and although we don't know much about each other yet, I find myself wanting to change that.

"We're getting together for Friends Night on Wednesday. We do it often; grill out, hit up Brodie's in town, and shoot the shit. We're heading to Brodie's this week for wings and beer. If you're free, you should come out with us."

She hesitates for a moment, circling a ring on her finger as she mulls it over.

"My son will be with his dad, so I can make it work. I'll just have to be back by eight when he gets home."

I smile. "Sounds like a date."

She nods, studying my smile. I have a sneaky suspicion she's searching for a sign as to how I feel about her being a mother, and if she thought it would steer me away, she's dead wrong.

"How old is your boy?"

"His name is Huxton, and he just turned five not too long ago. He'll be starting kindergarten soon."

"You'll have to bring him around to one of our Friends Nights. My sister, Layla, and cousin, Brit, both have kids and they often bring them along. It would give them someone to play with and keep the kids occupied while we all hang out."

Her eyes brighten up, and she grins, talking about her son and the mention of him making new friends.

"Oh, Huxton would love that." Her voice is lighter than it was a moment ago. She peers down at her hand, running her finger over the dark maroon nail polish.

I don't want her to be nervous around me, and I can sense something in our interaction from when we first were introduced to each other to now makes her hesitant.

I reached my hand out, wrapping my fingers around hers, hoping to calm whatever she felt in the moment.

"I'm looking forward to seeing you on Wednesday and having you both around more at our Friends Nights."

This time, she doesn't hold back. Her grin stretches across her face. I trail my eyes over the light dusting of freckles dotting her nose along the apples of her cheeks. It's hard to resist the urge to kiss her again.

I don't know her story, and I don't want to come on too strong, but I can't help wishing I could have another taste of those lips.

Now that I know how soft they are and how good they taste, it would be hard to be near her and think about anything else.

I check the time on my watch. I knew I needed to take off if I had any chance of making it on time for my shift.

"I need to leave for work, but I don't want to go," I whisper.

She didn't say anything, but I could sense something was on the tip of her tongue. I felt her thumb brush over the back of my hand. It was subtle, but it felt like a live wire jolting through my body.

"Two days."

"I'll be counting down until it's here." I wink.

She giggles and shakes her head. "Like I said, you sure know all the right things to say to a woman."

I remove my hand from hers, brushing back the strand of hair that fell forward, hiding her face. I trace my thumb along her jaw, below her lower lip.

God, it would kill me to walk away from her without kissing her again.

"It may be the right things, but more importantly, it's the truth."

chapter four

HAELYNN

"Huxton, are you almost ready? Your dad will be here any minute," I shout down the hallway toward his room.

I haven't heard a peep out of him since we got home. I'm about to head in there to check on him when he comes flying out of his room, his Spider-Man cape floating through the air behind him with a mask over his eyes.

"I'm comin', I'm comin', I'm comin'." He giggles, racing toward me.

I've been on edge all day thinking about him going with his dad tonight. Atlas called to cancel his time with him last weekend and couldn't bother to give an explanation, so he hasn't seen him in over a week.

Right now, our custody agreement is he sees him for three hours on Wednesday nights and every other weekend. The reasons I left still weigh heavy on my mind, knowing the monster I've seen him become over the years.

In the eyes of the court, I don't have any proof to show the damage he could cause our son by being around him unsupervised. It's my word against his, and I have a feeling it will be an uphill battle forever.

I hate that it's come to this, but I've witnessed the ugly he hides behind closed doors. I'll do anything to protect my son from him. It's the very reason I packed us up and walked away for good.

"Are you excited to see your dad?" I ask as he zooms past me into the kitchen, pretending to shoot his web as he swings from one side to the other.

He goes quiet for a moment and shrugs. "Why can't he come here and we can all be together?"

"I know, sweetie. He wants to spend time just the two of you."

"He's always cranky, though, or working."

My heart aches for him. I spent the last few years feeling the same way.

"His work keeps him busy sometimes, but he's excited to see you."

I knew he wanted to spend time with his son. I just wish he'd make their time together a priority.

"What are you gonna do? Won't you be all alone?" He pushes his mask up to the top of his head. Strands of his hair stick up through the eye holes.

"Don't you worry about me, buddy. Do you remember Madelyn and Alex from across the street?"

"Is that the Madelyn from work?"

"That's right." I smile. "I'm going to meet up with her and some of her friends for dinner. I'll be home when you get back, though."

His little lip puckers out, and his eyes dart away, avoiding me.

"What's wrong, Huxie? Talk to me." I bend down, reaching for his hand to pull him closer.

He pushes his mask off his head, letting it drop to the floor behind him, and wraps his arms around my neck.

I rub his back, soothing him. The past few months have been hard, and he's gone through so many changes—from being at home with me except for the couple of hours a day a few times a week he'd go to preschool and living with both his parents, to staying with grandma for a few months, to living in our own place.

Until now, if anything bothered him, he rarely let it show. I still can't help but let the guilt twist in my gut over the thought.

"I don't want to go."

His words are muffled against the side of my neck. I squeeze my eyes shut, hating the sadness mixed with the plea.

"Can't I just go with you? Please, Mom."

"Not this time, sweetie. I promise the next time they invite me over, I'll bring you along with me. How's that sound?"

He pulls back and nods. His lower lip puckers out, avoiding looking at me.

He sighs when we hear the horn honk outside. I grit my teeth to cover up how annoyed I am. Where could he possibly be in a hurry to go when he has Huxton for the night? It's like he can't be bothered to come to the door to pick up his son.

"It looks like your dad is here. I'm sure he has something fun planned for you," I say, hoping it's the truth. "Get your shoes on, and I'll meet you at the door."

The energy and excitement Huxton had flying around in his Spider-Man costume has all but deflated out of him. He grabs his shoes by the door, where he kicked them off when we got home earlier.

I spot the sleek black Audi parked along the curb in front of the house. The windows are tinted dark, making it impossible to see him. I don't need to, though. I can picture the snarl curling his lip. His gaze shooting daggers at the new home I got all on my own. Without him.

Pride washes over me thinking about how much he hates to see me living and raising our son on my own. He liked to remind me how I wouldn't be able to survive without him. Something about knowing I've proved him wrong feels like one step closer to taking back everything he stripped away from me over the years.

Atlas honks again, letting it drag out the second time. I clench my jaw, wanting to tell him off. I can only imagine how annoyed my neighbors are, staring out their window on our quiet street, but he doesn't care.

He'd turn up his nose at me and everyone else on the block, snubbing them like he's better than them. Arrogance doused in whatever bullshit response he'd have, too.

Huxton races down the hall, his mask in hand. He flashes me a smile, and I push the screen door open, following him outside. He gives me another hug and a kiss on the cheek before climbing into the back seat. Atlas doesn't bother to acknowledge me before he takes off down the street.

I stand in the yard, watching until they disappear from sight. I consider making the drive to Brodie's now, but I have time to kill before everyone is supposed to meet up at six, so I decide to make the walk instead. I grab my purse and remember to lock up behind me. It's a short walk, but it gives me time to myself, something I haven't had much of these days.

Arbor Creek is so different from what I was used to. Growing up in Chicago meant businesses lined the streets, and the sidewalks were bustling with people. I've learned most of the people here travel to Everton or as far as Des Moines for work. It's a quick trip, mostly highways leading you to where you want to go.

Taking a seat on the bench outside of Brodie's, I watch cars drive by with people passing through town. I still have about twenty minutes to kill when I spot a pickup pulling up outside, and Corbin climbs out.

He's dressed in a burgundy T-shirt, denim jeans, and weathered boots. His arms are tan, and his hair is mussed, almost as if he woke up and ran his hand through it. A spark gleams in his eyes, and he smiles an easy smile, causing my heart rate to speed up.

"I was hoping I'd be lucky and see you if I showed up early." He shuts the door behind him.

"I had nothing else to do after Huxton left with his dad, so I decided to make the walk here instead. It's beautiful out."

The sun hasn't quite dipped below the horizon, giving us another hour of sunlight.

"I agree." His eyes linger on me before he glances into the distance at the sky, turning a mixture of orange and pink. He goes silent for a moment before his gaze returns to mine once again. "Beautiful."

His raspy tone sends butterflies fluttering in my stomach.

"We can go inside and find a table if you want?"

I nod. He reaches for my hand, kissing the back when I slip my fingers between his. I purse my lips together, shaking my head, recalling the first time we met.

He is smooth, and he knows it.

"I couldn't help myself. I told you, I've been counting down the days."

I smirk and nod in agreement.

"I will admit, I've also been looking forward to tonight."

He flashes me a wink. I swear, the way he looks at me does crazy things to my heart. There's something about him, the initial connection, and the spark I've felt drawing me in.

He makes it easy to forget all logical thoughts when he's around, and when he's away, it's hard not to think about him.

I've thought about the kiss we shared over and over, replaying it in my mind. I've tried to convince myself it was only for the pictures. We were there to help Madelyn and nothing more. It didn't mean anything to him. We were like two actors performing for the camera.

Except, at the moment, it didn't feel like nothing. It was everything.

It reminded me of how long it'd been since I felt wanted or desired by a man. I don't remember the last time Atlas looked at me the way Corbin does. Like he wanted to eat up every inch of my body, making it slow and torturous until I was left begging for him.

He'd enjoy every second, too.

He presses his hand against the small of my back, guiding me into the bar.

Booths line the wall with a dance floor in the center and the bar along the back. It gives off a rustic feel with dark wood beams and iron detail throughout.

"You want to sit at the bar, or we can grab a booth?" he asks.

The way his eyes drink me in and the pull I feel between us draws me closer to him. I've never felt so beautiful from one look alone. It's given me a confidence I hadn't realized I'd lost.

Maybe lost wasn't the right word, but it had gone away for a while. But something about Corbin has brought it back.

His finger rubs along my spine. The warmth of his hand makes it hard to focus on anything else.

"Let's do a booth."

The bar is mostly empty. It will give us time to talk before Madelyn and Alex arrive.

He nods, hollering to the bartender that we're claiming our spot. They must know each other, when he responds with a mock salute.

I expect him to take the seat across from me, especially with it being the two of us here. When I slide into the booth, he mutters, "Nuh-uh," under his breath and motions for me to scoot over.

I turn my body sideways, pressed against the wall to face Corbin. He settles beside me, slipping his arm along the back of the seat.

"Now this is better." He winks, rubbing his thumb along my shoulder. "Although I wouldn't mind if you decided to curl up against my side instead."

I narrow my eyes at him playfully, and he shrugs as if to say "it was worth the shot."

"Why'd you decide to move and settle down in Arbor Creek?"

This conversation could take a few different directions. If he's as interested as he seems to be, I might as well shoot him straight. I half expected him to pull back when I brought up Huxton when we were talking after the photo shoot, but if anything, he only seemed more interested.

In fact, I was surprised and relieved when he encouraged me to bring him to their next Friends Night.

"I lived in Chicago until I was nineteen and got engaged to Huxton's father. He started a business in Everton, so moving back and being close to my family seemed like the right decision."

He listens intently. If the mention of Atlas bothers him, he never lets it show.

"We separated about three months ago. I was staying with my mom for a bit, you know, getting back on my feet. When I started looking for a place of our own, it seemed like the right choice to stay close by."

"I'm sorry to hear that," he says, clearing his throat. "About the separation. We never go into relationships, especially marriage, wanting it to end. I'm sure it hasn't been easy for you."

A weight lifts from my chest, like a heavy sigh of relief at his understanding. He made it so easy to open up to him.

"Looking back, even before we got married, I saw signs it wasn't going to last. Red flags I chose to ignore. My father wasn't around growing up. He had passed away before I was born."

"Damn," he mutters under his breath. Corbin adjusts himself in his seat, taking everything in before he turns back to me. He moves his arm between the two of us, reaching for my hand. I tangle my fingers in his, needing the lifeline.

"It was hard growing up without a father. I can't imagine how different my life would be if he had been here."

I've thought about it a million times leading up to and since our separation.

What if I had clung to my connection with Atlas for the wrong reasons? Did I stay with him because I loved him, or was it because I didn't want Huxton to be without his father, too?

"In the end, I wanted to make it work for our family. It took a while before I finally accepted it wasn't going to work out, no matter how hard I tried. It's better this way." I blink back the tears, recalling the conversation I had with Huxton before he left with his dad. "I truly believe it's better this way."

"I can't imagine how hard it was for you to pack up and essentially start over. It says so much about you and the woman you are."

"It's taken time to adjust to being alone. The nights when Huxton is with his dad are hard." Corbin squeezes my hand in his. "It helps that I've started to get to know people here and made friends, though. I'm not going to say it's gotten easier, but it's certainly brought light to a dark time."

I sigh, tucking my hair behind my ear. The server approaches us, and she seems to recognize Corbin. Madelyn mentioned his job in law enforcement after the photo shoot, so aside from being from a small town, it makes sense he's taken the time to get to know people in the community.

She takes our drink order and flashes me with a warm smile, assuring us she'll be back with those in a few minutes. Meanwhile, Corbin never moves to let go of my hand and neither do I. Not even when a text message comes through on his phone, vibrating against my leg. He uses his free hand to slip into his pocket, pulling his phone out to check who it's from.

"It's Alex. He said they'll be heading this way in a few minutes. He got tied up at work but is almost home to pick up Madelyn."

"Okay." I smile, resting my head against the back of the booth. I soak in the few minutes, just the two of us, before they get here.

"I know you don't know me, or any of us well, but I hope you know you're not alone now. Not anymore. If you need anything, even if it's a hand around the house or someone to spend time with when Huxton is away, I'll always be here."

My heart squeezes in my chest. As much as I want to believe him, I can't shake the feeling that once he realizes the depth of my pain, it will be too much for him, and he'll be long gone.

"You shouldn't make promises you may not be able to keep."

He narrows his eyes at me and shakes his head. "You've been let down in the past. I can see it, and I get it. Even if this never goes any further between us, I mean what I say. Give it time, though, and I'll prove I'm not going anywhere."

chapter five

HAELYNN

As I sit on the front porch step, thinking about Corbin and our time together tonight, I spot Atlas's Audi turning onto our street.

It dawns on me how this is only the second time I've been with Corbin, and I already have this giddy, excited flutter in my stomach. I never felt this way when I first started seeing Atlas.

Atlas opens the door and steps out, dressed in his black suit from his day in the office. It's such a stark contrast between him and Corbin, making it hard to remember what I ever saw in him in the first place.

Despite all we've been through, I'd never take back the gift he gave me in Huxton. I couldn't imagine my life without him.

I jog down the steps and cut across the lawn as Atlas opens the back passenger door and Huxton climbs out.

"Hey, sweetie," I grin. His eyes light up. "Did you have a good time?"

"Yeah, Dad took me to his work."

I force a smile as agitation creeps up my neck.

"That's good. I'm glad you had fun. Why don't you go inside and get cleaned up. Your jammies are laid out for you on your bed. Get changed and I'll be in to read to you, okay?"

The heat of Atlas's stare burns into my skin. My anger simmers beneath the surface, causing my blood to boil.

He only had him for three hours tonight, and he couldn't manage to stay away from the office for even one night. Did he honestly think this was spending time with his son?

Huxton takes off toward the house. Just when I turn back toward Atlas, Huxton stops in his tracks holding his stomach and says, "Can I have a bowl of cereal, Mom? I'm hungry."

"Didn't you feed him dinner?" I growl under my breath. Why is he asking for cereal at eight o'clock at night?

"We didn't have time. It was only going to be a short stop, but I got held up."

I shake my head, holding my hand up to stop him. I didn't want to get into this with him right now in front of Huxton.

"Of course, sweetie. Go get your jammies on, and I'll be inside in a few minutes to make you something to eat."

Huxton nods. He spins around and runs up the front steps into the house.

"Are you kidding me?" I grit out.

His brows shoot up, and his lip curls in annoyance, glancing around him. I know he hates when I make a scene in a public place and not where he could properly put me in my place the way he'd like.

"Excuse me?" he spits out.

"You heard me. You haven't seen him in almost two weeks. You take him for a few hours and can't even manage to spend that time with him? Let me guess, you took him to your office and shoved him in one of those board rooms, gave him a bucket of toys you've had since he was two years old, and told him to play for a bit? I'm sorry being a father got in the way. You'll have to save your trip to the strip club for tomorrow night."

The words are out of my mouth before I have a chance to stop them.

We both know it's the truth, although by the time I figured out what kept him out all night, I had lost all the energy to bother arguing with him.

"Excuse me." He takes the step toward me, shoving me against his car.

I never had any proof he was cheating on me, but if I did, it would be game over for him. He knows what this would mean for our divorce. Honestly, I don't want anything from him but out of our marriage. Not the house, not his money.

I want custody of Huxton and to be free of his torment.

He reaches for my forearm, using his body to hide the force of his grip as he dips his head near my ear.

"I don't know who you think you are, Haelynn, but I think you need to remember who the fuck you're speaking to."

His breath feathers across my skin, and I curl my lip in disgust.

"Let go of me, Atlas." I attempt to jerk my arm out of his hold, but his grip only tightens, causing me to groan in pain. Tears prick my eyes as I stare up at the hateful man standing in front of me.

"Please, Atlas, you're hurting me." I blink past the tears threatening to spill over, not wanting to let him see an ounce of weakness.

"I suggest you listen to her, or I'll have to step in and see that you do."

Atlas releases my arm, turning to peer over his shoulder.

"Are you okay?" Corbin asks, glancing over to where I'm clutching my arm against my body. My chest heaves, struggling to take a deep breath.

"Yes." I force a smile. "Thank you."

He nods. His face reddens, and his nostrils flare. This side of him is so different from the outgoing and lighthearted Corbin I've gotten to know.

"I think you should go," I say.

Atlas slips his hands in his pockets, widening his stance, trying to intimidate Corbin. Corbin shakes his head, crossing his arms in front of him. A grin curves his mouth, as if he's waiting for Atlas to test him.

"Did you hear that, buddy? She said you should go. This isn't any of your business. You can be on your way now." Atlas smirks.

"Atlas, I was talking to you."

My forearm throbs. I know without looking he's left a bruise. If he hadn't done this several times before, I'd think he damn near fractured my arm. It'll take a few days, maybe even a week, but I'll be fine. I just hate how hard it makes it to cover up in the sweltering heat of the summer.

Corbin raises his brow and shakes his head, turning his attention back to me.

"It's fine. I'm done here anyway."

He's not only talking about tonight. There's an underlying warning never to bring it up again, or next time, it'll be much worse.

I'm all too familiar with the subtle jabs and the hidden threats, warning me not to mention it or I'll regret it later. It was all a ploy to get me to play the role of his dutiful wife.

Except I don't have to listen to him or comply with his rules anymore.

He climbs into his car, slamming the door behind him and peels off down the road. When he's gone, Corbin cuts across the space separating us. I can tell it bothers him, and he wants to pull me into his arms. If I'm being honest, I wish he would too. It doesn't escape my mind that Huxton waits inside for me, and I need to check on him.

"Are you okay?"

"Yeah, I'll be okay. I'll have a bruise, but it'll be fine."

I wince, stretching my arm out. Corbin reaches out, brushing his fingers over the blue and purple forming under my tender skin.

"I know it's not my business, and dammit, I'm sorry, but I need to know, Haelynn. Has he done this to you before?"

It's not something I've talked about with many people. When I finally broke down and told my mom I needed her help, the floodgates opened, and I spilled it all.

Every last sordid detail of how I got to where I was now.

I hated how insecure and weak I felt to put up with this from him for all these years. What they say is true though, once you find yourself in this position, it's hard to walk away.

I stare back at Corbin, not wanting to admit the words out loud, and he curses under his breath.

"Damn, baby, I'm so sorry." His jaw clenches, and the muscles in his arms grow taut.

"I appreciate you being here, making sure I'm okay. I need to get inside and check on Huxton. I'm sorry."

His eyes flash toward the house. The sun has long since gone down. The only light comes from the streetlamps at the corner of the block and the few lights on the front of the houses.

"I understand," he says, slipping his hand down my arm, running his fingers through mine before he drops them at his side. "I'm going to say this again because I want you to know nothing's changed. If you need anything, and I mean *anything*, I'm here for you. You're not alone. You no longer have to put up with him or his scare tactics. You say the word, and I'll be here as soon as I can. Okay?"

I nod, not wanting to tell him I'd hate to get him mixed up with my problems again. Despite how great our time together has been, I know what kind of mess this could turn into if we were to continue down this road. If Atlas got any hint Corbin was more than some innocent bystander, he'd make my life a living hell.

All I want is to get through the next few months without further incident and convince him to finalize the divorce so I could move on with my life.

"Thank you," I whisper, giving him a weak smile before passing by him. When I make it to the front door, I glance back to find him watching me. He raises his hand, waving at me with that smile that makes my heart come alive again.

Huxton sits at the breakfast bar, his little arms crossed with his head resting on them, fast asleep. I hate to wake him, knowing he's so tired, but I'm relieved he missed what went down outside.

I don't want him to go to bed on an empty stomach, so I quickly make him a bowl of cereal and rustle him awake, promising to tuck him in when he finishes. He's fast asleep as soon as his head hits his pillow fifteen minutes later.

I opt to spend a little extra time on self-care tonight, deciding to take a bath and get some reading in before I head to bed myself. I'm curled up in bed with my Kindle when a subtle buzz comes from my nightstand, pulling me from my story.

Corbin: Hey, it's Corbin. I'm sorry, I know I should've asked you first, but I begged Madelyn for your number. I just wanted to check in to see how you're doing.

I smile, pressing my phone against my chest.

Haelynn: You don't have to be sorry.

Haelynn: I'm doing okay, lying in bed doing some reading. Thank you for everything tonight and for checking in.

Corbin: You don't need to thank me. Now you have my number. If you need anything at all, I'll be there.

I stare at the screen, wondering what he looks like at this moment, trying to picture his face in my mind. I glance over at the empty space in my bed, picturing what it'd be like to go to sleep next to him.

Corbin: *Good night, Haelynn.*

Haelynn: *Good night.*

CORBIN

"You better have donuts or get the fuck outta here," Alex shouts, pointing toward the door when he sees I'm showing up empty-handed.

I'm on my lunch break and decided to drop into Compass Security to catch up with the guys. It's been an uneventful day, which I'm always hesitant to acknowledge out loud. It's a curse that always comes back to bite you in the ass.

Gage took over running Compass Security after his dad decided to step back. It was important to him to keep the business going, and Gage didn't hesitate to follow in his footsteps after he was discharged from the Navy.

"You'll have to get up off your ass and get some yourself."

I slip my hands into my pockets and nod toward Gage, who's sitting behind his desk, his head in his hands, staring at papers strewn out in front of him. His brows furrow, a pensive look etched on his face. I was waiting for the moment he'd inevitably pop a blood vessel in his forehead.

"What's up with you?" I ask.

"Nothin'," he mutters under his breath, not bothering to look up at me.

Alex's gaze bounces between me and back over to Gage. He shakes his head and shrugs, just as baffled as I am by his mood.

Gage and Alex recently spent time in Virginia Beach working on a large drug trafficking operation. This was important to both of them, but to Gage, it was personal.

His dad spent his career going after men funneling drugs from Virginia through the Midwest. He lost Gage's uncle when word got out he was behind a sting operation gearing up to take down two of the biggest drug lords in the area.

He hasn't said much about what went down while they were away. He was there to do a job and wasn't the type to get distracted from his mission. Alex let it slip he had spent time with some girl while he was away. When shit went down, Gage found out she was only using him to find out what he knew.

He isn't handling it so well.

Alex swore me to secrecy, so as much as I want to ask him about it, I can't. I'm stuck dealing with his cranky-ass moods, waiting for his inevitable crack.

"I hear you had a run-in with Haelynn and that soon-to-be ex-husband of hers," Alex says.

Gage's head perks up at the mention of Haelynn. Dropping the papers on his desk, he narrows his eyes on me. Alex laces his fingers behind his head, tilting back in his chair.

"What do you know about that fucker? He seems like a real piece of work," I question.

"Not much, honestly. We stopped by to help her the day she was moving in. She told Madelyn she left her husband and, up until then, had been staying with her mom."

I'm relieved Haelynn is across the street from them. Once Madelyn considers you a friend, there's nothing she wouldn't do for you. Haelynn and Huxton included. I trust Alex will keep an eye on things too. It's just who he is.

I get the feeling she needed more of those type of people in her life. It also makes me feel better to know she'd have someone close by looking out for her.

"Madelyn came home and hasn't stopped talking about how great the photo shoot went. It seems like the two of you hit things off."

He wiggles his brows, flashing me a playful wink.

"If I didn't know better, I'd think she was holding out on me," I joke.

Alex leans forward, resting his elbows against the table. "Yeah, Madelyn told me things were heating up between you two."

"I'm not gonna lie. There's definitely a spark there."

I've replayed the moment when I turned around to see her standing in front of me a million times and haven't been able to get the sight of her out of my mind. I've never felt anything like it. We hadn't even spoken to each other, yet the magnetic pull between us was so thick it was intoxicating.

Haelynn went from being tense and uncertain to melting in my arms. I want her to feel safe and comfortable, free to be herself. As time ticked by, she warmed up to me.

I've been living the life as a single bachelor for too long. The dating pool in Arbor Creek is small, especially when you know too much about the skeletons living in everyone's closet.

I'm not one to judge. Hell, Lord knows my family has been the talk of the town a time or two. If my parents have taught me anything, it's that there's a lot more to people than what meets the eye.

I've grown up with damn near most of the town, though. I can't remember the last time I felt anything near the way I feel being near Haelynn.

I haven't been able to stop thinking about her. I considered dropping by or shooting her a text message to check in with her. She just moved to town, and with a son, she likely has a lot on her plate along with getting settled in. I don't know where she's at, but I don't want to make a move too soon and lose out on a chance because she's not ready.

"Madelyn came home trying to convince me to take some sexy pictures with her."

Alex lifts his finger to his mouth, pretending to lick it before circling his nipple. I lift my fist to my mouth, choking out a laugh.

All the while, Gage doesn't even crack a smile. It's like the sense of humor he once had was soaked right up out of him.

"What do you even know about this girl anyway?" Gage asks, his voice cutting through the room, flipping the mood upside down.

I narrow my eyes at him. "What's your problem?"

"I don't have a problem." He shrugs. "I'm just trying to figure out how this girl drops into town, and you haven't considered doing your due diligence to check her out."

"Is there something you want to share with me? Feel free to enlighten me."

He shrugs again. "It's not on me to do. All I'm saying is you don't know this girl or what her past entails. Maybe you should keep your guard up for more than two seconds before you start trippin' over yourself trying to get her attention."

I sense there's somethin' he isn't telling me, but whatever's on his mind is dropped when he reaches for the stack of papers sitting on the desk, effectively ending the conversation.

I glance over at Alex, who shakes his head, seemingly as dumbfounded as I am.

I've tried several times to get Gage to talk to me, but he always shuts me down. I want to tell him to cut the bullshit already and tell me what his problem is, but that's the thing about Gage—it's always on his time.

If you try to push him, the harder he'll push back.

I guess I'll give it time and wait things out. He'll come around and talk to me, eventually.

"I'm gonna dip out," I mutter. My lunch is over anyway, and I need to get back to work.

Alex told me he'd hit me up later, and Gage left me with nothing but a head nod as I walked out the door.

The rest of the afternoon was much like the start of my shift. I stop down at the station to punch out for the day before I swing into my sergeant's office to check in.

I knock on the doorframe and stick my head in. "It's quittin' time for me."

"How was your shift?"

"Low key. Mostly traffic stops, although I did get a call from Danny up at Brodie's asking me to swing by Sutton's place. I guess he hasn't been in all week."

He chuckles, leaning forward to press his elbows against his desk.

"I had to remind him just because he hadn't been into the bar isn't cause for me to go peeking my head in on him, but I stopped by to check on him. I guess he's been sick for a few days."

"That's Arbor Creek for ya," he jokes.

Only in a small town would a call come in to the police to do a welfare check on someone simply for not coming into a bar for a few days. I understood Danny's concern, though. Sutton is getting up there in age. His wife passed away last year, and his family lives out in California.

People around here look out for each other, which is a nice way of saying they like to stick their nose into everyone's business. They have good intentions, though.

I tilt my head and flash him a wave, heading back out to my truck parked in the employee parking lot.

I haven't spoken to Haelynn since our text exchange the night we went out to Brodie's for Friends Night. I told her I was here if she needed me, and while I hoped she'd take me up on the offer, I also got the feeling she would hold me to it when I said I'd prove to her I wasn't going anywhere.

I'd give her space, but I don't plan to back down just because her piece of shit ex was trying to mark his territory.

In case he hadn't remembered, they separated for a reason.

Me: Hope you're having a good day. Tell Penny not to work you too hard.

It is still early in the day, and I know she has a couple of hours left before her shift ends.

Haelynn: Like a dog!

I hit the call button, and a second later, when the line connects, her soft voice filters through the phone.

"Are you trying to get me in trouble now?"

"I guess it depends. What sort of punishments are on the table?"

She giggles. "You sure are a handful, you know that?"

"So I've been told." I chuckle, loving the sound of her laughter. "I won't keep you too long, though. I just wanted to check in and see how you've been doing."

She pauses. "I appreciate it. I'm doing okay, getting settled still. Huxton starts school in a couple of days. Easing us in with a half week. We have Back to School night tonight. I'm not sure who's more nervous, though, me or him."

"I can imagine, but it'll be good for him. Get him out there and make new friends."

"He's ready for it. Me, on the other hand? The jury is still out."

"Well, I meant what I said about you bringing him the next time we get together. We're grilling out this weekend over at Madelyn and Alex's place. The kids will be there. Bring him with you. It'll be a good time."

"He's supposed to be going with his dad this weekend," she said. There's a rustling on the other end of the line. I picture her sitting at her desk, phone pressed against her cheek. "Although, if I'm being honest, I'm fully expecting he'll back out like he did the last time."

Annoyance laces with her disappointment. My lip curls, recalling the way he spoke to her and his smug expression when I walked up on them.

I've seen his type before. I don't want Haelynn to know I've been sticking my nose in her business, but she's right. His record is spotless, but it doesn't mean I didn't notice all the calls to their residence.

The reports never mentioned any domestic violence, only that Atlas had been heavily intoxicated and belligerent. The neighbors were always worried about Haelynn and Huxton, wanting to make sure they were all right.

"We'll grill out again soon. Even if he can't join us this time, we'll make sure to get him to the next one. He'll have a good time with Layla and Brit's kids."

"He'll love that."

Haelynn pauses, and silence falls over the line, leaving only the soft sound of her breathing.

"I haven't been able to stop thinking about you all week," I murmur.

"Me either." She sighs. "Five days."

I want to ask her if I can come by one night before then after she puts Huxton to bed. I know how it would sound, though, and I don't want her to get the wrong impression.

I also know she has a lot going on right now. Like I said before, I'll go at her pace.

I'm not going anywhere.

chapter seven

HAELYNN

It's taken some time, but we've started to get into a routine at home, just the two of us. I was worried about what the separation would do to Huxton, but seeing how well he's adjusted, how we both have, I wish I had made the decision sooner.

We attended Back to School night at Huxton's new school last night. I think I was more worried and nervous than he was. You would've never known he was the new kid with how easily he jumped right in, playing with the other kids while the parents listened to the teacher talk through what was in store for the upcoming year.

As hard as it is to think about Huxton being in kinder-garten, I am happy to know he'll be staying busy while I am working, and it gives him the chance to make some new friends.

It's been almost a week since I've seen Atlas. Aside from a few text messages over his plans to take Huxton tonight, we've hardly spoken to each other.

The old Haelynn would've dropped it and let it go. Over time, I've learned not to bring it back up, knowing it would only make things worse. It's as though he doesn't want to remember the way he's treated me, and mentioning it is like poking a bear.

I'm standing in the kitchen, stirring the pasta in the pot on the stove, when Huxton comes barreling down the hall. His dad will be here in about thirty minutes. I shouldn't worry about it, but I decided to fix him dinner before he left, not wanting a repeat of last week.

"Did you have a good day with Gram?"

Huxton doesn't answer me for a minute, his eyes following the remote-control car he's driving around the kitchen, navigating it between my legs before looping around the other side.

"Yoohoo, did you hear me?"

He tilts his head up toward me while never taking his eyes off his car.

"Maybe it's time we put the car up," I suggest.

He quickly follows it up with, "No, please."

I shake my head and smile, repeating the question.

"Yeah, she took me to the library, and we picked out a few books. It was kind of boring after that."

He drives the car toward him, picking it up and turning it off. After setting it on the counter, he climbs up into his seat.

"You only have a few more days before you start school. Are you excited?"

He bounces in his seat, a smile spreading wide. His curly brown hair mimics the same movement.

"I'm excited." He grins. "Ms. Layla was really nice."

We don't have much time before his dad will be here. The oven timer goes off, and I quickly pull out the chicken nuggets, tossing a few on the plate before adding a side of macaroni and some sliced apples. It's not ideal, but it'll do in a pinch.

His eyes light up when I set his plate down in front of him, and he digs in. Right as I reach for a dishrag to wipe up the counters, the doorbell rings.

"You finish eating. I need to talk to your dad." I motion with my finger for Huxton to sit, walking down the hall toward the door.

Atlas reaches for the handle to the screen door and steps into the entryway, not bothering to wait for me to let him in.

He wears a steel gray button-up shirt and black slacks. His hair is styled neatly, reminding me of the uptight businessmen I used to see walking the streets of Chicago. He pulls his sunglasses off slowly, letting his eyes travel down my body, doing a scan of what I'm wearing.

His jaw clenches, and his eyes narrow. I know full well whatever condescending comments he's going to make will be his jealousy rearing its ugly head, or he'll be an asshole despite trying to cover it up.

"He ready?" he asks.

"He's eating. He was hungry, so I thought I'd take that off your plate tonight."

He shakes his head, clearly not liking my response.

"We need to talk about the other night." His words come out softer, clashing with the stoic look on his face. I don't know if it's possible for someone to show two personalities at the same time, but he does. I've learned to walk on eggshells around him for this reason.

If I make one wrong move and misread him, it could turn out to be my greatest mistake.

"Okay," I say, glancing down the hall toward where Huxton remains sitting. He's pulled out one of the books he checked from the library and is flipping through the pages. He dunks one of his nuggets in ketchup before taking a bite.

Relieved he doesn't seem to be paying us any attention, I turn my focus back on Atlas.

"What do you want to talk about?"

"I wanted to apologize," he says, the last word coming out higher than I believe he intended, signifying how unlike him it is to say such a thing. I don't remember the last time Atlas apologized to me, much less for putting his hands on me.

"Can you clarify? What is it you're sorry for exactly?"

He rubs his thumb over his chin, glancing at Huxton before turning his attention back to me.

"You know I would never want to hurt you, Haelynn. It's just... this past year, things have been so stressful. Between work and the move."

When he talks about the move, he's not talking about me moving to Arbor Creek. He's referring to when we bought our last house together. I personally didn't find it necessary for us to move again. The house was even farther away, adding another thirty minutes to the drive to see my mom. Huxton would have to transfer schools, meaning he'd go to his second preschool in the past two years.

It was closer to his job, though, and much like everything in life, it's what Atlas wants or nothing at all.

We weren't given much of a choice, so when I saw the opportunity for us to get out and make a break for it, I took it.

"You know, you can blame it on whatever you want, but it's not what led us here. It was inevitable. It's time you come to terms and accept it."

"So this isn't your way of trying to get my attention. This is what you really want?"

I exhale an exasperated sigh. I can't even wrap my head around the mindfuck that is Atlas and everything he's trying to say right now. The constant change, never knowing what to expect, always sitting on the edge of my seat waiting for the moment he inevitably bursts.

"Yes, Atlas." I pause, folding my arms in front of my chest before dropping them to my side. I'm not going to cower away from him anymore, not when I felt like it was finally my time to stand and show him I'm serious. "Yes, this is what I want."

He scoffs, shaking his head. Whatever nice guy act he was trying but failing at putting on disappeared.

He stares past me into the living area. His eyes eat up the old, worn couch my mom passed down to me with the loveseat on the opposite side. The wood floors are scratched and beat up. I've told myself that once things settle down and I find time, I'll polish them, and they'll look good as new again. The walls remain bare. No pictures or decor, leaving them a stark white against the dark-brown sofa.

It may not look like much to him, but it is ours, and what's important is we feel safe here. It's our home, and even if he wants to look down his nose at me, he can't take it away from us.

"What, you think you can leave, take my son, and move into this hole in the wall? Do you honestly think you'll be able to keep this up with all the legal fees coming your way?"

A knot in my stomach twists, the taste of bile rising in my throat.

"Excuse me?"

"Don't play games with me, Haelynn. C'mon. Do you really think you can run away and I'll do, what? Nothing? Sit here and watch you play house while you're secretly trying to convince a judge to give you sole custody?"

"I'm not doing this with you right now. You're here to take your son for the night." I look down the hall at Huxton. "He's ready to go. Go enjoy your time with him."

I move to walk past him when Atlas reaches out, grabbing my arm to stop me. I grit my teeth, wincing in pain from where he left a bruise the week before. I yank my arm away from him, clutching it to my chest. His eyes widen, darting up to meet mine.

"Shit, Haelynn, I'm sorry."

The lost look on his face is mixed with sadness and despair. He wants me to forgive him, but I don't think I can. He's put me through so much pain and heartache leading up to now that I don't have anything left to give him.

My fingers hold my arm, massaging it to ease the pain.

"Atlas, I don't know why you keep saying you're sorry when I don't think you truly know what you're even sorry for."

I close my eyes, shaking my head, not wanting to even get into this with him again.

I know he loves Huxton, and I believe a part of him loved me, too. While I expected him to grovel when he realized what he lost, I didn't expect it to last for long.

Atlas isn't the type of person to put himself into a position to make him look weak. Although I would argue there's nothing weak about a man who can own up and admit when they're wrong, he doesn't see it that way.

He'd hide behind whatever lie he was using this time, convinced he had nothing to be sorry for before he'd ever apologize with genuine emotion behind it.

"The best thing you can do now, for you, for Huxton, and for me, is to focus on being a father. Okay?"

I'm waiting for the moment when he returns to being Jekyll and Hyde, throwing me through a loop on which side he is now. When he looks past me, down the hallway toward Huxton, I'm surprised when it doesn't come.

"Yeah..." He trails off. His eyes grow distant before he turns back to me. "Yeah, okay. I can do that."

I nod, forcing my mouth into a thin line. I drop my arm, not wanting to give Huxton any cause for worry.

Atlas doesn't say anything more as he watches Huxton grab his backpack, shoving his books in it, before joining Atlas at the door. Huxton turns back to me, lifting his hand in a small wave. Atlas follows suit with a nod, holding the door open as they both duck outside.

It's not until the door shuts behind him that I'm able to release a heavy sigh, and the tension of facing him again lifts off my chest. In the back of my mind, I know it's still only a matter of time before things shift again, and Atlas is back to being the man I've always known him to be.

Sooner or later, we'll break free.

chapter eight

CORBIN

"There he is." Layla sighs, throwing her hands up dramatically when I open the door to Oh My Goodies.

My cousin, Brit, owns the small-town bakery. Between this and the gas station at the end of the road, it's about the only place you could go nearby to get a fresh cup of coffee. I'm certain Layla and I are single-handedly keeping her in business. I rarely miss a day of stopping in before my shift, not to mention I'm addicted to her apple cinnamon muffins.

"You say that like I'm running late. It's not even eight o'clock yet, which is when I told you I'd be here."

Layla can be a bit theatrical and has been since the day she was born. She's the youngest out of the three of us kids. When they found out I was a boy, my dad made a promise to my mom they'd try again for a girl. Layla was the only one of us who went overdue. She wailed for a solid fifteen minutes until my dad stepped in and held her.

Our dad always joked he was surprised she didn't grow up to be a singer with the pipes she had on her. I guess he was on the right track. She put her theatrics to good use as the elementary school music teacher.

Since I returned from the Navy, we've made it our weekly routine to meet up for coffee before heading off to work. Brit always makes it a point to prepare fresh apple cinnamon muffins for me. Like the good cousin I am, I'll often take a couple of extras off her hands.

The small crowd this morning meant only a few people were in line ahead of us. I spot Will and his wife, Phyllis, seated in the booth near the front. He had owned a car repair shop until about six months ago when he decided to close their doors and retire.

He raises his hand and tilts his hat, nodding his head in a greeting.

When it's my turn, Brit slides my coffee along the counter toward me and sets a paper bag next to it with what I assume are my goodies.

"Am I really that predictable?" I grin.

She shrugs. "Have I ever been wrong?"

"Well, there was that one time..." I trail off, joking.

Brit shakes her head and rolls her eyes. I toss a twenty on the counter, and she snatches it away, punching a few buttons on the register before the drawer pops open.

The doorbell dings, and I spot a wave of chocolate curls in my periphery. Even if I hadn't noticed her walk in, I certainly would've felt her presence.

My eyes lock with Haelynn. Her footsteps falter, standing in the doorway until the door closes, pushing her inside. She lets out a small yelp, caught by surprise, before pressing her lips into a firm line to hide her smile.

She does a quick glance around the diner to see if anyone heard her. I shrug, reassuring her it wasn't a big deal.

"You know her?" Layla whispers under her breath.

"I'll be right back," I reply, waving to Brit to keep my change. I swipe the bag and coffee off the counter, then cross the room toward Haelynn.

"I guess it'll be a good day after all." I grin, stepping in close to her. The move stirs up the air between us, and I breathe in the smell of her perfume mixed with the clean scent of her shampoo.

"Smooth talker," she murmurs playfully.

"It's the truth. I woke up this morning still thinking we had three days left. I've been counting them down, but seeing you now makes it a bit more bearable."

"You come here often?" she asks, taking a step forward to join the end of the line.

I nod, peering over toward Layla and Brit. Although Brit was busy taking orders, I wasn't blind to the curious glances they threw our way. I recognize their inquisitive looks, speculating what was going on between the two of us.

When I turn back toward Haelynn, her eyes bounce from Layla and back to me. She presses her lips into a straight line, adjusting her purse on her shoulder.

"You could say I'm a staple around here," I joke. "That's my sister and cousin over there... gawking."

The tension on her face relaxes. "I recognized her. It took me a second to figure out where, but I think I saw her at Huxton's school the other night."

Layla, who's busy listening in like a hawk, slips through the line toward us.

"Well, hello." Layla smirks, her eyes moving from me, over to Haelynn, and back.

"Ignore my brother. He must've lost his manners. I'm Layla." She extends her hand between us to shake Haelynn's.

Brit greets Haelynn with a smile as Haelynn introduces herself to Layla. I'm surprised she knows Brit already.

"Haelynn works for Madelyn over at Memories and Moments," Brit clarifies, and I nod. "We met when I took the twins in to get their pictures taken."

"How do you know each other?" Layla asks, pointing between the two of us. She presses her lips together, trying to smother the grin threatening to stretch across her face.

"Madelyn asked me to do a favor for her down at the studio."

I know once I tell them about our photo shoot, they'll ask a million questions we don't have time to answer. I'm more focused on getting a few minutes alone with her.

"Uh-huh," Layla says, trying to figure out what's going on between us. "Well, Ms. Haelynn, if you didn't know, my brother is single. He's a great catch."

I cover my mouth, trying to contain my laughter.

"He's got a great job with benefits, a house he pays for, and no crazy baby mommas out there for you to worry about," Layla jokes.

Haelynn joins in with my laughter at the mention of no baby mommas. I'm thankful she doesn't seem to be taking her comment personally when we both know her ex would fall in that category himself.

"He's sweet, caring, and the best uncle around." I raise my eyebrows in surprise.

"I said around, chump. Cool it. Once Liam is back in town, he'll be making a run for that title."

I chuckle, nodding in agreement. "You're right, you're right."

Haelynn puts in her order with Brit while they chat about the twins and how great the photo shoot went.

"We'll actually be bringing the twins with us to Madelyn and Alex's place this weekend. You should come by with Huxton," Brit mentions.

Haelynn peers over at me and smiles. "We were just talking about grilling out the other day. Huxton will be with me this weekend, so it works out perfect," Haelynn says.

I notice her subtle way of acknowledging Atlas backed out like she suspected.

"I need to take off to get to school, or I'll be late." Layla hugs me. She turns to Haelynn, telling her how great it was to see her again, then waves goodbye to the group as she slips outside.

Brit has a line of customers forming out the front door, so we duck out behind her. I'm thankful for the opportunity to have a few minutes alone with Haelynn. She clutches her bag along with the coffees for her and Madelyn in her hand.

"Here, let me take that off your hands." I reach for her bag, holding it along with mine. We stroll out the front door over to the small parking area.

She points at her car parked just a couple of spaces from mine. I follow her, reaching to open the door.

"How was Huxton's first day of school?"

She leans over to set the drinks inside before turning to face me. It's hard to read her expression. She looks lost in thought, but there's a mixture of sadness there too.

"Is everything okay?"

"Yeah." She brushes her hair away from her face. "It's good, really. It's a big step, and watching him go is hard."

"I'm sure it's not easy, especially as a mom, but it's good for him. Think of all the fun he's having and the new friends he'll make."

She smiles. "Oh, he is. I heard all about it over dinner last night. I wasn't expecting to get emotional until you brought it up. It's just, his dad never even checked on him last night to ask how his first day went. But you... you remembered."

She blinks through the tears forming in her eyes, sucking in a deep breath to collect herself.

I set my coffee down on the hood along with the food and take a step closer to her. I've missed touching her. Seeing her upset now, I can't resist the chance to pull her into my arms. She comes to me easily, wrapping her arms around my waist.

"Thank you," she whispers. Her words are muffled against my chest.

I run my hand over her hair, and her body relaxes, her arms tightening around my waist.

"I know I joke how you always know the right thing to say at the right time. I'm not used to it. You pay attention and notice the little things. A part of me wants to pull back and question everything, but when I'm around you, I just... I can't."

"Good," I say, pressing her back against the car door. "I don't want you to pull away. I understand you're hesitant and, at times, may want to run. I'll go at whatever pace you're comfortable with, but I'm not walking away."

"You say that, but what if you change your mind? What if we let this go further, and you realize you bit off more than you could chew with me?"

I tuck a strand of hair back from her face and brush my thumb lightly along her lower lip. My dick hardens at the sight of her running her teeth over it, her tongue trailing to wet the dry skin.

"It's not going to happen. Neither of us can say for certain what the future will bring." I sigh, my eyes pausing on her lips again. "When you're around me, all I can think about is wanting to be closer to you. I want to touch your soft skin and feel your body pressed against me. I want to listen to you talk about anything and everything you'll tell me."

"I've never felt anything like this before. I get it's soon, and I understand you're scared, but I'm not."

"Where have you been my whole life?" she jokes. "Why hasn't some woman come along and snatched you up already?"

"I've been here, waiting for you."

chapter nine

HAELYNN

Corbin and I exchanged a few messages over the past few days, but after the confrontation with Atlas, I had a lot on my mind. I put all my energy and focus into taking care of Huxton and my job.

I remember how fast I fell for Atlas. Corbin came out of nowhere and has tipped my whole world off its axis. Although he's nothing like Atlas, I still can't stop thinking about how quickly it all happened, and all the questions have started to swirl around in my head.

At times, I'll be sitting at my desk and glance over at the bed staged in the studio not far from me, and just like that, he's consuming my every thought.

I left work early yesterday to talk with my lawyer about the divorce proceedings. I hate how ugly this will turn once

Atlas finds out I'm moving forward with fighting for sole primary custody of Huxton.

Atlas was well known in the Everton area. After his grandpa passed away, his will stipulated that a large chunk of money was to be put into a trust for Atlas. He's always been a smart businessman, so when he turned twenty-five and gained access to the funds, he put every cent into building his own brewing company.

The media praised him for being one of Iowa's youngest and fastest-growing entrepreneurs. Although my lawyer agreed that I should be awarded custody, she cautioned me that we'd have a hard time convincing the judge to sign off.

On paper, Atlas was the picture-perfect husband and father, and he had the coin to put up the fight.

The last thing I want is to bring Corbin into this mess, especially when it's only just begun.

Madelyn and Corbin invited me to Friends Night and encouraged me to bring Huxton. The urge to pass on the offer was there, out of fear of where this would go with Corbin, worrying it wasn't the right time to introduce him to Huxton. I've pushed so many people out of my life over the past few years because of Atlas.

I'm not going to let him control my life anymore.

"Will there be other kids to play with too?" Huxton sighs, shoving his feet into his sneakers, then bending down on his knee to lace them up.

"Well, Ms. Layla will be there. She's friends with Madelyn, and she said she was bringing her daughter with her too. I believe her cousin will also be there."

Huxton's eyes light up, and he purses his lips together, attempting to smother his grin.

Oh boy, why do I think one day this kid will give me a run for my money when it comes to girls?

"That's cool, that's cool."

He pretends to play it off, jumping to his feet. Checking his appearance in the mirror, he turns his head from side to side, using his hand to smooth an unruly curl into place.

I shake my head, leaning against the wall opposite him with my arms folded in front of me. What have I gotten myself into?

"You almost ready there, Rico Suave?"

He scrunches his nose. "Rico who?"

I chuckle and push myself off the wall. I wave him over, urging him out the door.

"Don't worry about it now. It'll make more sense when you're older."

We lock up the house behind us, crossing the front yard and the street over to Madelyn and Alex's house. I immediately spot Corbin's pickup truck and a few others parked near the end of their large driveway.

The voices and laughter grow louder the farther we get up the driveway toward the backyard. A deck with a large patio sits off to the side with a smaller picnic table lined with drinks. Towels and sandals are discarded, like they were too excited to bother caring where they ended up. I spot a group of kids near the back with a massive bouncy house Corbin promised.

"Good thing I wore my swimmin' trunks, huh?" Huxton's eyes light up, pointing at the sprinkler.

"I'll run home and grab a towel for you to dry off with when you get done. Go play. Have fun, and remember—" I say before he interrupts.

"I know, Mom. I know! Be a good friend." He flashes a grin before taking off.

"Haelynn," Madelyn sings, shooting out of her lawn chair. They're in a circle around the bonfire pit with coolers positioned between them like makeshift tables.

She waves at Huxton as he zooms past her. She takes off after him before spinning around, waving at me again.

"You don't have to worry about him. Layla brought her daughter, and Brit brought the twins with her. He'll have a great time."

I spot Corbin behind her, standing with a group of guys. I try to play it cool and not stare too hard. I swear I can feel his eyes roaming every inch of my body.

I recognize Alex among the group, but the other guy is new to me. He has a light stubble lining his jaw, and his eyes are dark. You can tell he's not someone to be messed with, and I'm not sure what to make of him.

When my eyes meet Corbin, he flashes me a wink before letting his gaze trail down my legs, pausing before finally meeting mine again. He subtly rakes his teeth over his lower lip.

I'm terrible at reading lips, but I swear he just muttered, "Fuck," under his breath.

"Grab a drink and join us." Madelyn slides her arm in mine, leading me to one of the larger coolers.

While we're walking, Madelyn makes conversation. "I went into the office to finish editing the photos this morning. I'm so excited for you to see the final product. I think you'll love them."

I don't doubt I will. I've been dying to sneak a peek, curious how they turned out. Madelyn offered to let me see them unedited, but I told her I wanted to wait, and she could surprise me.

She's incredibly talented behind the camera. Word has started to swirl about her skills, and business has been picking up at the studio. It's only the beginning, and things will take off for her before we know it. I can just feel it.

The mention of the photo shoot has me giving in, peering over my shoulder to where Corbin is standing. He notices me eyeing him and heads our way. Alex and Mr. Serious follow him.

"You made it." Corbin grins, slipping past Madelyn to greet me. He wraps his arms around my waist, pulling me in for a friendly hug. Madelyn's brows shoot up, and her eyes gleam with pride at her matchmaking skills.

Corbin leans in near my ear and whispers, "You look beautiful."

"I'll grab you a drink." Madelyn chuckles, motioning to hers that she needs another.

Corbin does a round of introductions, including Mr. Serious, whose name is Gage. It isn't until Corbin mentions my name that I notice his demeanor change. He tilts his head, and his gaze looks through me as if triggering a memory, but he's not quite sure where to place me.

Except I don't recognize him at all.

"Madelyn mentioned you just moved across the street from her..." Gage asks. His tone is flat, devoid of any emotion.

Corbin's body goes stiff. He's drinking his beer and pauses his hand midair, seemingly confused by Gage's mood.

"Yes," I respond before biting the inside of my cheek.

"What made you decide to settle down in Arbor Creek exactly?"

"My mom is from here originally, and it seemed like a good place to raise my son."

"Your mom?" he questions, raising his brows. I'm confused where he's going with this.

Corbin jabs him on the arm. "Dude, what's your deal?"

"Nothin' man. I'm simply curious about who she is and why she's all I hear about all of a sudden."

"Why don't you chill a bit?" Corbin pushes Gage back, muttering under his breath to go grab a beer.

My face turns red in embarrassment. It wouldn't have been so bad if it wasn't for the condescending air to his questioning. Almost as if he felt like I wasn't good enough to be among them, and I couldn't think of the slightest reason.

Who is he to judge me or question my intentions? He doesn't know anything about me.

Madelyn hands me a bottle of water, knowing me well enough to know I wouldn't be interested in drinking with Huxton there. I take a step back from the group, my eyes moving to where Huxton's running toward the sprinkler. You could spot his beaming smile from a mile away.

"I'm going to run across the street quick to grab Huxton a towel and a change of clothes." My eyes do a quick scan around the group. Brit and Layla, both smile, reassuring me they'll keep an eye on him for me.

"I can join you," Corbin says, slipping past Madelyn. "I need to, ah, grab something from my truck quickly anyway."

Alex mutters, "Liar," between a cough. He shrugs as his whole face spreads into a smile. Not the least bit bothered by being called out.

"We'll keep Huxton occupied. Don't hurry back now." Madelyn giggles, flashing me a wink. Corbin takes my water and sets it on the table, leading me toward the driveway where we first came through.

I glance down at his T-shirt with "Navy Veteran" printed across the front.

"I didn't know you were in the Navy." I smile, peering at him from beneath my lashes. "I'm not surprised, though. It makes sense."

"Why is that?"

"You seem like the type of man who would fight for our country. Loyal, honorable."

He ducks his head and murmurs, "Thank you."

"Is that how you met Gage and Alex?"

He shakes his head. "My parents have been friends with Madelyn and Gage's parents since before we were born. They still are to this day. We grew up running around this town together. Alex met Gage serving overseas and the two became thick as thieves. He offered him a short job working at Compass Security, so he moved to Arbor Creek for a few months. Well, he met Madelyn not long after and the two of them fell in love."

I nod along with him, smiling at the mention of Madelyn and Alex falling for each other.

"Listen, I'm sorry about Gage back there. He can be a little gruff sometimes, but he comes from a good place. You'll see, I promise. He's just been through some things, and, I don't know, he hasn't been himself lately."

Corbin reaches for my hand, tangling his fingers in mine, and gives them a squeeze.

The sun is starting to set, turning the sky a mixture of orange, pink, and purple. It's still warm, but the further the sun disappears, the cooler it will get.

We dash across the street and up my driveway toward my front step.

"You can come inside if you want. I should only be a minute. I just need to grab a few things for Huxton quick." I pull the keys from my pocket and unlock the door.

Corbin holds the door open and follows me inside, standing near the entryway. He glances around, taking in our home before his eyes fall on mine.

I hold up my finger, signaling I'll only be a second. It's not until I'm in Huxton's room, shoving his things into a bag, that I realize I finally have Corbin alone and all to myself.

As much as I've tried to distance myself from him, I can't help but think about how badly I've wanted to kiss him since the day of the photo shoot. When we ran into each other at Oh My Goodies and he walked me to my car, I could've sworn he was going to kiss me.

I've wanted his lips on mine so damn bad. The day of the photo shoot had only been a taste, but it was enough to drive me wild.

chapter ten

CORBIN

I stand in the entryway, my eyes scanning the collage of photos hung on the wall, ranging from when Huxton was born to his first day of school.

When I was texting with Haelynn earlier this week, she mentioned spending time one night hanging up some pictures she recently had printed. After seeing all of Madelyn's hard work, she started to get inspiration for some of her own photos of her and Huxton.

There's one of the two of them outside of his school. She's crouched on the ground next to him, a wide smile on his face, missing his front tooth. She's glowing with happiness, and I make a mental note to try to keep that smile on her face as often as possible.

She rounds the corner, and I step back from the wall, turning toward her. She has a small blue bag slung over her shoulder. Her eyes bounce from me and over to the photos on the wall.

"He looks just like you." I gesture to the picture of them I had been studying.

"He does." A thoughtful smile curves her mouth.

She takes a step closer, adjusting the strap on her shoulder. A foot or so remains between us, but I'm unable to resist her. I reach out and grab her hand, pulling her into my arms. I can't pass up the chance to be near her, especially now that I have her all alone.

"Do you know how badly I want to kiss you right now?" I whisper, our fingers tangling together. Her body relaxes. She shrugs the bag off, letting it drop to the floor near our feet.

"How much?" She bites her lip, and her eyelashes flutter.

I trace her jaw, brushing her hair out of her face. Leaning in, I press a soft kiss against her lips and mutter, "Fuck," at the taste of her.

She laughs and tilts her head back, gazing into my eyes. She glides her hand around the back of my neck, urging me to kiss her again. This time, when our lips connect, I don't hold back.

The front door is open behind us. The sunlight filters through the screen door, although it's fairly shaded as the sun has started to set.

I take a step backward, leaning against the wall, and pull her along with me. I grip her hips and spin her, caging her in, earning me a yelp in the process. She tilts her head back and laughs as I go in for the kill, kissing along her collarbone and nipping her skin until I reach her earlobe.

"You drive me wild with how badly I want you," I groan.

She tilts her head to the side in a silent invitation, and I take it. I'll fuckin' take everything she's willing to give me. Since I walked into the studio, I haven't been able to think about anything but her.

Her hands find mine, and our fingers tangle together. I raise them above her head, pinning her in place. When I ease up to make sure I haven't pushed it too far, I'm ready to collapse to my knees at the sight of the desire glossing her eyes. Her lips are red and swollen from mine.

She bucks her hips toward me, and goddamn, she's a sight to see.

"Tell me," she mutters, catching me by surprise. "Show me."

She's as sweet as she looks, but the sound of her enticing me with her dirty mouth has my dick so damn hard it's impossible not to want her right here.

"Tell you what, beautiful? What do you want to know?"

"Corbin," she moans when I step in close, lifting my thigh between her legs. Her small denim shorts have been teasing me, showing off those toned legs. Her blotchy red chest tells me she's feeling this as much as I am.

"Say it," I urge her, capturing her mouth in another kiss. She squeezes her eyes shut. So when I pull back, it takes her a second to blink her eyes open and focus on mine.

"What do you want?"

Her throat bobs when she forces a swallow, and her eyes lose focus, gazing past me.

"It's been so long since I've felt wanted like I do when I'm around you." She sucks in a deep breath. "I want you to show me how badly you want me."

"Fuck," I groan. Releasing her arms, I hike her leg over my hip. I tip her chin up, wanting her eyes on mine when she feels how badly my body craves her.

When I grind my dick against her, it takes everything in me not to come at the sound of her moan bubbling up from her chest. If she wanted to know how I felt, if she needed validation of how badly my body aches for her, I'll give it to her. I'll never let her forget it, either.

"You feel this, Hae?" I ask. Her head rolls back, her hands clutching onto my arms, holding her up. "If I wasn't worried about half your neighborhood, including our friends, seeing us, I'd be on my knees in front of you right now."

Her eyes flutter, and she thrusts her hips toward me once again.

"Is that what you want?" I lean in close, whispering against her ear. "Is the thought of me touching you turning you on?"

"Yes," she chokes out.

I release her leg, letting it drop to the floor, and trail my fingers over her hip. Her tank top is pulled up, her tanned skin teasing me above her shorts.

I brush my finger along the edge of the denim, barely caressing her soft skin. Her body trembles with need as I flick the button of her shorts.

"Are you sure?"

Her eyes burn into me, staring down at where I've paused my hand at her waist. I release the button of her shorts and slowly unzip them, leaving them sitting low on her hips. I spot the black lace of her panties, my finger skimming over the thin material.

"Corbin," she whispers, adjusting her stance to open her legs farther for me.

I slip my hand down the front of her pants, rubbing her pussy. Her wetness coats my skin through the material. Her grip on my shoulder tightens when I brush my finger over her clit.

"Oh God," she moans, tilting her head back against the wall.

I'm trying and failing at keeping my cool. My dick strains against my pants, begging for a taste.

I quickly glance out the door, wondering how easily someone could look inside and see us before I say, "fuck it." My knees hit the floor in front of her, and her eyes bulge open in shock.

"Slip your shorts off, baby."

She quickly looks outside, checking to make sure no one is around.

"I promise, I won't let anyone see us. There's no way you can see in with how dark it is in the hall."

She rakes her teeth over her lower lip before shimmying her shorts down, letting them drop on the floor in front of me. She's left standing with only her panties on.

I reach up and let them glide down her legs too, leaving her bare in front of me. The sight of her standing here, glistening with desire, makes it impossible not to want to taste her.

I adjust her leg over my shoulder and use my fingers to spread her open for me before swiping my tongue over her swollen bud. Her body trembles, and her leg goes wobbly.

Using one hand to hold her steady, I tease over her folds with the other before sliding a finger inside her.

She's so wet and tight. All I can think about is how good it would feel to have her wrapped around me, but I push that thought out of my mind. I want to soak up every minute, focusing on her and her pleasure.

"Corbin," she moans, raking her fingers through my hair, gripping the strands in her fist.

I groan, leaning forward to trace through her folds before sucking her clit into my mouth. The combination of licking and sucking mixed with the slow and steady rhythm of my finger has her hips jutting toward me, growing more urgent and frantic as she chases her release.

"Let me taste you," I murmur while I trail kisses up her thigh and over her mound, feathering my warm breath over her heated skin.

When I finally reach her pussy again, I swipe my tongue over her clit and curl my finger, massaging the bundle of nerves. Her body trembles, and I alternate between suction and licking, sending her soaring over the edge.

Her body twitches, and her legs shake beneath her. I do everything I can to keep her standing upright while not stopping. She releases a heavy breath, sagging into my arms, and I hold her against me.

We sit here for a few moments while she attempts to catch her breath, her arms wrapped around my neck. When I help her to her feet, she pulls her panties and shorts back on, and smoothes her shirt back into place.

She attempts to run her fingers through her mussed hair, taming the locks back into the well-put-together woman she was before.

She reaches her hand out toward me, cupping her small hand over my dick.

"We can wait," I whisper. "There's no rush, Haelynn."

She jolts her hand away, attempting to smooth over her reaction, but not before I catch the hurt on her face.

"Whoa, hey, what's wrong?"

"I'm sorry," she blurts out. "It's not... it's not you or anything you said. I think sometimes I forget how a healthy relationship should be."

I narrow my gaze, trying to decipher what she's trying to say.

She winces, her face turning red in embarrassment. She reaches her hand up, massaging her fingers over her forehead.

"I guess you could say I'm not used to being with someone who's selfless about my needs. It's always been tit for tat. I scratch your back, you scratch mine sort of thing."

"Your pleasure is my pleasure, Haelynn. I get just as much out of watching you come for me as you do. It will never be about me wanting or expecting something in return. Do you understand?"

The more I get a glimpse into the type of person her ex was, the less I like him. This is yet another reason on an already long list of why he makes my blood boil.

The fact he would make her feel like she owed him something simply for pleasuring her makes me sick.

I don't know how he could call himself a man.

I tug her into my arms, sliding my hands around her waist. She reaches up to cup my face and kisses me.

What was once heated and full of passion is now slow and sensual, and I pour everything I feel for her into our kiss. I know it's too soon to be certain of what this is exactly, but it's unlike anything I've ever felt before.

I've been in love, but it was back before I joined the Navy. It was different, though, and nothing like this. All I want to do is wrap her in my arms and never let her go.

God, I pray I won't ever have to either.

chapter eleven

HAELYNN

Corbin and I head back to the bonfire after we snuck away for a bit. Huxton never seemed to notice I left. He was too busy running around and jumping in the bouncy house to pay me or anyone else any mind.

I found myself more and more attracted to Corbin as the night went on. He is so different from what I'm used to. The way he carries himself and how he interacts with Huxton. A warmth spread in my chest at the sight of them playing catch and when he taught him how to throw the ball properly. Huxton's eyes lit up when he got it down.

When the sun disappeared from the night sky, the bonfire truly kicked off. Madelyn busted out leftover sparklers for the kids from their Fourth of July party the month before. We roasted marshmallows and made s'mores while we reminisced on our days in high school.

I learned Corbin played football his junior and senior year, after his coach found out about his throwing arm. The more he shared, especially when he got to talking about his time in the Navy and following in his brother's footsteps, the more I believed he was too good to be true.

At one point during the conversation, I brought up living in Chicago and how different small-town life was compared to the big city. It didn't escape my notice the way Gage's eyes stared emotionless into the fire, but judging from how he clenched his jaw and flared his nostrils, I knew he was listening.

I can't quite figure out what it is about me or the topic of conversation that makes him seem on edge. I tried to remember what Corbin said earlier about how he was going through some things, reminding myself he's only looking out for his friend.

The next day is a Sunday, and I have a list of things to get done since yesterday was no work and all play.

"We're going to make this a quick trip, okay? In and out," I say, peering into the rearview at Huxton.

I pull the car into the parking spot outside of the hardware store in the center of town. I don't know if they're going to have the part I need, but I'm desperate at this point.

I have no desire to make the drive to Everton, but if I need to, then I guess it's what I'll have to do. It's what I get for thinking I can trust someone to sell me a working lawn mower on Craigslist.

I groan under my breath and snatch the keys from the ignition, tossing them into my purse. I do a quick once-over in the mirror and cringe at the sight. My hair could use a wash, and dirt covers my hands, with a matching streak across my face.

Let's just hope I don't see anyone I know. This is when it comes in handy not knowing anyone, even when living in a small town.

I sling my purse over my shoulder and hit the locks, urging Huxton to stick behind me so we can make this quick. He squints his eyes, staring up at me. He must sense my stress over the situation because he doesn't say anything, although I know a comment waits on the tip of his tongue.

"Thanks for being my big helper today, bud," I mutter when he reaches his hand up to take mine.

It's true, he's been sitting on the ground, trying to help me while I figured out what the hell is wrong with the stupid thing. These are the times I wish I had someone to call for help. A father, someone, anyone. My mom wouldn't have the slightest clue what to do. She'd toss some money at me and tell me to call a handyman or to cut my losses and buy a new one.

She's helped me enough as it is, and the last thing I want is a handout. So instead, I spent the last hour scouring YouTube for videos to narrow down the issue, landing on it being a new carburetor.

I have a feeling the small hardware store won't have what I'm looking for, but I'm crossing my fingers that luck will be on my side today. My yard is half mowed, and it's already four o'clock in the afternoon. At this rate, it'll be after seven if we had to make the drive into town.

I reach in my purse and feel around for the paper I shoved in there when we ran out the door with my short shopping list of the things I'll need.

"Stay with me, Huxie."

"I am," he mumbles.

I'm too busy reading the signs above each of the aisle, not paying attention to where I'm going or who's walking toward me when a man comes hightailing it around the corner. We're both moving quickly, and he comes up on me fast, causing us to nearly knock heads as we crash into each other.

"Oh my gosh! I'm so sorry, I should've been paying more attention." I wince, my toe taking the brunt of the beating. I swear I could feel the crunch of my bone beneath his steel-toed boots.

"Corbin," Huxton exclaims, full of excitement.

"Hey, buddy." He grins, reaching his arm out toward me. He's holding a hose in his hands. For a brief second, my mind flashes to the scene in *Fifty Shades of Grey* when Christian is out buying toys for his red room.

My thoughts go completely out the window, distracting me from the pain radiating up my foot.

"You okay?" He checks me over, looking down at my foot. "Dammit, I'm sorry."

"It's okay." I grit my teeth. "I'll be fine, just gotta walk it off. Right, Huxie?"

"Dats right. Sometimes ya gotta walk it off." He grins.

I chuckle, watching his little head nod enthusiastically.

"What are you two doing here?"

"Mom broke the mower," Huxton blurts out. My eyes snap over to him, silently telling him to zip it.

"Is that right?" Corbin chuckles, glancing from Huxton over to me, obviously noticing my attempt to keep him quiet.

"How'd that happen?"

"I guess it was my lucky day, and I bought it that way."

His brows furrow, not appreciating my attempt at humor. He's right, though. My misery wasn't funny.

"I bought it online and met some guy to pick it up earlier today at the gas station in town. I was more worried about meeting him somewhere safe and in a public setting. I didn't even bother to check to make sure it worked. Got a few rows mowed on the front yard before it crapped out on me."

Corbin winces, shaking his head. "Honestly, if it did that when you got it home, it probably would've worked at the gas station, anyway. You wouldn't have known either way. You can't beat yourself up over it. Do you know what's wrong with it?"

"My trusty YouTube research has me thinking it could need a tune-up or it's an issue with the carburetor."

"I'm not sure you'll find what you're looking for if it's the carburetor, but I can swing by my place quick and grab a few things if you'd like a hand. At the very least, I can get you fixed up for today so you can finish mowing. How's that sound?"

He tosses the hose in the air, catching it before flashing me a big smile and wiggling his brows at Huxton.

"Yeahhh!" Huxton cheers. "Can I help too?"

"Of course, you can! I'm going to need all the help and muscles I can get."

Huxton releases my hand, flexing his muscles to show them off to Corbin. He crouches to check them over, giving them a squeeze before he nods in approval.

"I think you're just the man for the job."

I giggle, noticing the happiness glowing on Huxton's face. My heart soars seeing the two of them together.

Corbin stands and glances over at me. "I just gotta pay for this quick. I'll swing by my place to load up my mower and grab a few tools, and I'll be right over. Give me fifteen, maybe twenty minutes tops."

"Are you sure? I hate to take up your Sunday evening. I bet you have other things you'd rather be doing."

"Are you kidding? There's nowhere else I'd rather be," Corbin insists, finishing with a wink.

I peer over at Huxton, wondering if he caught it. He flashes me a smile, and I know he did.

"All right. We'll see you there, then."

The entire way back to our place, all I can think about is Corbin coming over. Huxton fires off questions and then proceeds to tell me how he's going to show him his Spider-Man mask. When we pull into the driveway, I spot Madelyn outside in her yard too. She shouts over at me and waves, carrying a couple of shopping bags into the house.

"Let's hurry up. I need to get cleaned up."

"Yeah, you need to wash your hands and wipe the dirt off your face."

Thanks, kid, for looking out.

I quickly wash up and freshen up while I'm at it. I do a quick sweep of the house, telling Huxton to pick up the Lego blocks he dragged out earlier and left scattered on the floor before I forced him outside with me.

I don't expect Corbin to come inside, but if he does, I don't want the house to look a mess.

A few minutes later, I hear his pickup pull up outside, and the nervous flutter I get in my stomach when he's around returns.

"You smile a lot when you see Corbin," Huxton says, staring at me. He still has a pile of Lego blocks on the floor in front of him, doing more playing than cleaning up.

"You better get back to work, or Corbin's going to wonder where his partner in crime is."

He sighs, scooping a handful and tossing it into the little Rubbermaid tote.

Corbin wears a black T-shirt with the sleeves cut off and a pair of denim jeans. I can't imagine why he'd want to wear jeans in the heat of summer, but damn, does he look good in them. He pulled on a baseball cap since he left the store. He's going to make it hard to focus on anything but him.

His arms flex when he reaches for the handle of the tailgate, lowering it before jumping onto the truck bed to grab a few tools.

"I'm going to go see if Corbin needs any help. Once you're finished, put your sneakers on, and you can join us."

I slip outside, letting the screen door slam shut behind me, announcing my presence. Corbin looks up, twisting his baseball cap around backward, giving him a better view of me.

"You need any help?"

"I think I got it, but I wouldn't mind the company."

I smile and nod. The combination of his backward cap and the outline of his muscles flexing, covered in his tattoo sleeve, has me practically salivating at the mouth. Sweat dots his brow, and I nearly choke when he lifts his shirt to wipe his face, showing off his stomach.

Corbin was stocky and built like a linebacker. He didn't have those chiseled abs you'd see on the front cover of *Sports Illustrated*. He had meat on his bones, and man, did he have me wanting a taste.

He wouldn't have a problem lifting me in his arms and carrying me right into the house.

The sound of his throat clearing, peering up at me from under his dark lashes, earns me a devious grin.

"What were you thinking about?" he asks, just as Huxton comes barreling out the front door.

"Hey, buddy." He quickly changes the subject, his gaze still lingering on me. "Want to give me a hand? I could use one."

Huxton kneels on the ground next to him, tilting his head down to look beneath the mower while Corbin gets to work. I smile warmly at the sight of them.

Corbin may have it all down in the looks department, but watching him with my son, seeing how patient he is while talking through each step, may be the most attractive side of him I've seen yet.

chapter twelve

CORBIN

It didn't take long for me to figure out what was wrong with the mower. It turns out it wasn't the carburetor; it just needed an alignment, which isn't too difficult to fix. Once we got the mower running, I encouraged Haelynn to tackle whatever else she had on her to-do list for the day. She hesitated, insisting she could take it from here.

When I insisted I wasn't leaving until I took care of it, she shook her head and wrapped her arms around me in a hug. Nothing serious. It was no different than if Madelyn were to stop over and help her with something around the house.

When she pulled back, the blush that tinted her rosy cheeks had me wishing I could pull her back for more.

She invited me to stick around for dinner as a thank-you. I ran home to get cleaned up and met them back to eat. We decided to eat out on the patio, enjoying one of the last few warm summer nights. Fall is around the corner, and soon, the leaves will change, and the evening temperatures will turn brisk.

I remain in the kitchen while Haelynn tucks Huxton in for bed. She apologized when she added it would be a few extra minutes while she read to him. I didn't want to take her time away from him, but I also didn't want to miss out on the chance to get her alone.

I haven't been able to stop thinking about the night of the bonfire. The way her body came alive when I touched her. I crave all the subtle ways her body reacts to me.

She's my addiction, and I never want to let her go.

I understand it hasn't been long since she separated from Atlas. The last thing I want is to push her too hard and ruin what we have forming between us, but I also want her to know I'm not going anywhere. If I have to take things slow and move at her pace, I will.

I recognize the quiet sound of a door clicking shut and her soft footsteps padding down the hallway. The sun has begun to disappear beneath the clouds. The sliding glass door leading out to the patio is left open, leaving only the chirping of the locusts in the distance.

She smiles as she rounds the corner and sees me standing there, waiting for her. It's almost as if she had expected me to slip out, leaving her to tuck Huxton in, but was happy to find me still here.

"I don't think he'll be waking up anytime soon."

"Yeah?" I ask, quirking my brow.

He was a big help while I was fixing the mower and took care of cleaning things up when we finished. Guess that means he'll be sleeping well tonight.

Haelynn changed her clothes since earlier in the day, now dressed in a red silk tank top and shorts with a white sweater wrapped around her. The summer sky turned the air cooler when the sun disappeared behind the clouds, blowing a fresh breeze through the open windows.

There's a softness to her features, a vulnerability seeing her dressed in her pajamas, standing in front of me in the quietness of her house. The kitchen is dim, the only light coming from the end of the hallway, bathing us in darkness.

She peers up at me through her long lashes. The look in her eye makes it difficult to contain the urge to pull her into my arms again.

"I bet you're tired too." She sighs, folding her arms at her waist. "You were so wonderful with Huxton today. I can't tell you how much I appreciate all your help."

"I told you if you needed anything, I'd be here."

She nods, a smile threatening to break across her face. "You did. I'm just not good at asking."

"I figured, but you should know, Haelynn, I want to help. I want to hear from you, for you to lean on me if you need anything. I want to get to know you more and for you to trust me."

Uncrossing my arms, I brace my hands against the counter behind me. Her eyes drop down to where my hands clench the granite. I notice a change in her breathing, the subtle rise and fall of her chest beneath the dull lighting.

Seeing how her body reacts to my words, I push off the counter and take a step toward her, then another, until only a foot remains between us.

"I'm not going anywhere, Haelynn. Not unless you tell me to go."

In my mind, I'm talking about the future, but in a way, I'm also talking about tonight. I don't want to leave. The thought has me nearly coming out of my skin with need.

"Good," she whispers, glancing at the floor as if working up the courage. She drops her hands to her sides and straightens her shoulders. "I don't want you to go either."

It was all the permission I needed. My hands slip around her lower back and reach down to grip her thighs, lifting her to sit on the edge of the counter. Her arms wrap around my neck, holding on as my lips crash down on hers.

She moans subtly against my mouth, opening her legs to grant me better access. I want to be closer to her in every way possible.

I pull back, and her eyes flutter open, her lips swollen from mine. I swear, this woman makes me feel like a horny teenager with my cock pressed hard against the seam of my zipper.

"Haelynn," I croak. "I'm sorry, maybe we should slow down tonight?"

She winces, and I reach my hand out to stop her.

"No, it's okay. I get it. I understand," she mutters and pushes my hand away from where they're gripping her thighs, moving to slip off the counter.

"You understand what exactly?" I ask, stopping her from walking away from me.

"Listen, I've spent the past four years with a man who's hardly touched me. I've gone to sleep at night wondering what it is about me, picking apart everything about myself, wondering why I wasn't good enough for him anymore. When we're together, one thing leads to another, and before I know it, I'm back in your arms. I don't want to go down this road again only to feel like I'm not good enough, especially for a man."

A part of me wants to pump the brakes, hating how she could so quickly push me away and think I'd ever not want her.

"How could you even think that?"

Her brows furrow. "Well"—she sighs—"why did you stop then?"

"Stop?" I rake my hand over my face and through my hair. "I don't want to stop. Hell, if I had it my way, I'd carry you down the hallway to your bedroom. That's the point I'm trying to make. Look at me right now." I blink slowly, motioning to the obvious bulge in my shorts.

"My body can't help but want you. Don't you get it? I know what an asshole your ex was. He mistreated you and took for granted what an amazing fuckin' woman he had in front of him. I just don't want to ruin this before we have a real chance to see what this could be."

She looks past me, her eyes growing distant for a moment before they find mine again. She reaches out toward me, her hand turning into a fist as she stops midway before dropping it against my chest and releasing a heavy exhale.

"I don't want to think about the past, the future, or what could happen if this were to go wrong. I don't want to think about anything. I want to forget it all and just feel your hands on my body. Can we do that? Even if it's for one night."

I know what she's asking for, and as much as I wish our first time together were different, I understand what she needs right now.

The thoughts swirling through my mind leave me quiet, and she must misread my response, shaking her head and moving to step away again.

"Please stop walking away from me."

She doesn't say anything but doesn't move any farther, either.

"I told you I wasn't leaving. If you need me to take care of you and pleasure you in ways your body hasn't even begun to imagine, I will. I'll give you that and so much more. There won't be an inch of your body left untouched. You'll ache for it as much as I do, and there's no doubt you'll come back for more."

Her eyes flutter, a haze of desire glossing over them. A grin curves the edge of her mouth, sucking in a deep breath.

I grip her arm softly and turn her to face me. Tucking a strand of hair behind her ear, I cup her chin. When I dip down to press a soft kiss against her lips, it starts out slow and full of passion. Her fingers skate over my chest, gliding them up to wrap around my neck, her nails dragging over my skin.

I pull back and nip at her lower lip, capturing it between my teeth. She lets out a deep moan mixed with the muffled sound of my name.

The throaty sound unleashes something deep inside me. I grip her hips in my hand, once again lifting her. This time, she moves her legs to wrap around my waist.

I cross the dining room and down the hall. I pull back, trying to watch where I'm going. Her lips skate over my heated skin, nipping along my neck as she goes.

"Which door?" I whisper, but it comes out more like a growl.

She grinds against me, and I dig my fingers into her ass, trying to hold her still. I'm trying to keep it down, not wanting to wake Huxton. I'm not ready to stop now.

"Last door on the right."

I race down the hall, using my elbow to push the door open and shut behind us before crossing the room to drop her on the foot of the bed.

She giggles as she falls back, her sweater falling open, exposing the matching red silk tank top underneath. She's not wearing a bra, and the outline of her nipples peek through the thin material. My eyes zero in on the taut flesh, and she moans, appreciating how my eyes eat her up.

"My God, you're so fucking sexy."

Blush highlights her cheeks, matching the color of her top. I crave watching all the ways her body comes alive for me.

That ex-husband of hers didn't know what the hell he had in a woman like this. She's rare and so fuckin' beautiful.

She stands, shrugging off her cardigan, and drops it on the floor next to her. She reaches for the hem of her top when I stop her.

"Let me." I cover my hand with hers, raising the material over her head.

The rose color of her cheeks matches the soft bud of her nipples. If I thought I was hard before, I'm practically coming out of my pants now.

She fidgets, holding off the urge to cover herself up, but she doesn't. With the soft glow from the lamp on her nightstand, I have enough lighting to enjoy taking in every inch of her body.

Her skin is smooth, my fingers skating over her curves as I kneel before her, slipping off her shorts next. I glance up at her, and she grips my face in her hands, pressing a kiss against my lips.

When she releases my mouth, I brush my lips over the faint marks on her stomach. I suspect they're from when she carried Huxton.

"Corbin," she murmurs, raking her fingers through my hair. I tilt my head back to look her in the eyes.

"You're beautiful. Every single inch."

chapter thirteen

HAELYNN

Corbin dips his fingers into my waistband, tugging the material over my hips, letting it drop to the floor. When he spots my lace underwear, he quirks his eyebrow and asks, "Did you wear these for me?"

How do I tell him I was hoping this is where it would lead?

"Maybeee..." I drag out.

"Mmm," he moans, pressing his face against my mound. He inhales deeply, muttering under his breath about how good I smell.

"Oh my God," I exhale harshly, collapsing onto the bed.

Corbin stands. Reaching for my panties, he pulls them down my legs, then spreads me open for him. His eyes burn into me, staring at my hair fanned around me, over my body, and down to my pussy.

I've never felt so wanted by anyone before. When I was with Atlas, I was always modest, but it was really because I felt uncomfortable with him. He never looked at me like Corbin does. It's as though he can't get enough. His eyes eat up every inch as if he doesn't know where to start but wants to devour it all.

He unbuttons his shorts and drops them on the floor. He quickly whips his shirt over his head, standing in front of me in a pair of boxer briefs.

His hair is mussed. I drag my eyes over his body, a breath hitching in my throat at the sight of the tattoo that spreads across his chest, blending into the sleeve down his arm.

It's the first time I've seen it. He doesn't move, letting me take in the sight—the tribute to the honor and sacrifice he made serving our country.

He slips his thumbs into his briefs, pushing them down his legs, before standing back up. He oozes confidence, and the sight of him as he crawls up the bed and leans over me will forever be engrained into my memory.

He slowly runs his hand over my calf and up my inner thigh. He hitches my leg around his waist, brushing the tip through my folds, guiding himself toward my entrance. My body trembles with how badly I want to feel him on top of me, inside me, anywhere, everywhere.

"You're so wet," he groans, brushing the tip over my clit. He reaches between us, gripping his length in his fist, pumping it twice before smacking the head over my pussy.

I bite down on my lip in an attempt to smother the moan.

I stare at him through hooded eyes when he licks the pad of his thumb before rubbing it over my swollen bud.

He lightly teases me, stroking me until my hips take over, desperately searching for more.

I grip his face in my hands when he leans over me, capturing his mouth in a soul-searing kiss. His eyes roll closed when he slips inside me, releasing a low growl. He presses his forehead against mine. My body trembles beneath him, and he slowly pulls out before his hips piston back into me.

Something about this moment, the emotions coursing through me, causes my breath to get caught in my throat. I'm scared if I blink or close my eyes even for a second, I'll wake up and this will all be a dream.

Corbin coming into my life and everything about this night, the way I've felt in his arms from the first day. Even though neither of us said it, I could feel the love between us, and as happy as he makes me, it scares me too.

Corbin leans back on his haunches, guiding my leg over his shoulder, and pulls my body closer to him before driving into me. The change in positions hits the right spot.

He rolls his eyes shut, his breath coming out in heavy pants.

"Haelynn," he moans, staring down at me.

"Please don't stop."

I reach my hand between us, rubbing my fingers over my clit. His eyes blaze into me, watching my movements while thrusting in and out.

"I'm not stopping," he grits out. "I won't ever fucking stop."

He grips my waist, flipping me over onto my stomach in one swift movement. I toss my hair over my shoulder, tilting my head back to look at him, arching my back in the process.

His arm wraps around me, pulling me until I'm seated on his thighs. His chest molds against my back, and I grind against him. He nips and kisses along my collarbone and neck before sucking my earlobe into his mouth. His fingers tweak my nipple while simultaneously circling his hips beneath me. Both moves drive me wild with need.

I lean my head back on his shoulder, gliding my hand over his arm and lacing our fingers together, holding him to me.

"You feel so fucking good," he murmurs.

He pushes me forward on all fours, gripping my ass in his hands. I moan at the loss of him, sticking my ass out toward him teasingly.

"Hold on." He squeezes my ass in his hands before smacking my skin. The burning sensation sends a jolt through my body.

"Spread your legs open more."

He sends me reeling at the subtle brush of his fingers over my swollen clit before his fingers disappear once more. I want to beg him to stop torturing me when he grips my ass in his hands, spanking me again.

"My God," he moans, running his tongue through my folds from behind. I've never had my pussy eaten from this position. I lift my ass in the air, desperately seeking more.

"Mmm," he groans, pulling back before plunging back inside me in one swift move. His body folds over the top of me, pinning me against the bed. His hips swivel when he hits me deep.

Each time he pulls out, I rock my body back toward him, meeting him thrust for thrust.

I slip my fingers between my legs, brushing them over his dick before rubbing my clit.

"I'm close," he mutters. "I can feel your pussy milking me."

"Corbin," I moan. "I'm almost..." I pause, unable to finish the sentence.

Our movements grow frantic and chaotic with need until we're both sent crashing over the edge.

Corbin wraps his arm around me, pulling me with him as we collapse on the bed. I've never felt anything like this before and don't know how to recover from it.

Corbin eventually slips out of bed, and I whisper he can use the bathroom off my room, pointing toward the door. He's back at my side a moment later, urging me to roll over, helping to clean me up before dropping the towel into the laundry basket and climbing back in bed with me.

With his body molded against mine, our legs tangled together, and his arm wrapped around my waist, we fall asleep together.

Never, in all my life, have I felt as safe as I do in his arms.

HAELYNN

When Monday rolls around, I'm still walking in a daze, feeling the effects of my night with Corbin. I haven't been able to stop thinking about it since he snuck out before Huxton woke up.

I grip the door handle to the studio, pausing to let out a heavy breath, trying to shake myself from my thoughts before I head inside. If Madelyn picks up on something being amiss, she'll ask questions I'm not sure I'm ready to answer just yet.

Music blares throughout the studio when I walk in. I can only guess she showed up here early this morning to get some editing done. She tends to crank her music up when she's trying to focus. We've been busy recently with sessions, and she warned me she'd be pulling some crazy hours to get caught up.

"Haelynn? Is that you?" she shouts from the back before the music cuts off.

"Yeah, it's me."

I drop my purse on my desk, falling into the chair while I wait for my computer to boot up.

"Oh my God, I have something to tell you. I've been watching the clock waiting for you to get here."

She comes racing out of the room, her heels clicking on the floor.

"What's going on? Is everything okay?"

"It's more than okay. It's amazing! I need to show you this."

She looks at my computer screen, pausing when she sees it loading before reaching into her pocket to pull out her phone. Her fingers fly over the screen before she shoves it in my face, urging me to look.

"What am I looking at exactly?" My brows furrow, scrolling through a bunch of comments before my eyes land on photos of me with Corbin from our stranger shoot.

My mouth drops open. "Are these *the* photos?"

"Yes, scroll down. Look at all the comments and shares. You're frickin' viral, Haelynn! People all over the world are gushing over you and Corbin in these pictures. It's up to almost a half a million likes and thousands of shares. Can you believe it?"

Am I surprised people are seeing the talent Madelyn has behind the lens? Not at all. Am I shocked by the response to the photos of me and Corbin? Abso-frickin-lutely.

I never thought of myself as photogenic, so I couldn't believe it when she suggested doing the shoot with me, of all people.

It wasn't until I scrolled through the pictures that I got chills. There were endless comments from people who all seemed to think the same thing I had from the moment I met Corbin.

The connection I feel when I'm near him is unlike anything I've ever experienced in my life. It's hard to describe how I feel, and seeing people pick up on it through our pictures has tears pricking my eyes.

"Wow, this is amazing. I'm so happy for you!" I gush, shaking my head in amazement when I pass the phone back to her.

"Right! It's unreal. Not to mention, I've had countless messages and emails from people from other states and cities around Iowa who want to schedule a session with me."

My chest expands, knowing how hard she's worked and how much this means to her.

"You're kidding!"

"Not at all. I had to turn the phone on out of office this morning just to focus on editing. I had over ten calls before nine, and we weren't even open yet. I could hardly keep up with it all. I don't know what I'd do without you."

"That's incredible, Madelyn. You deserve this!"

"Thank you, but I should be thanking you. It was you and Corbin they fell in love with. I just helped bring you two together."

Warmth spreads over my cheeks, and Madelyn giggles. "You're blushing."

"I know, but it's just... I can't help it. It's crazy. It feels like it was just yesterday I moved here, and so much has happened in a short period. I never expected to meet someone.

I can't remember the last time I was this happy. I'm almost scared to admit it out of fear of losing it, but it's the truth."

"You glow when you talk about him. Even when I walked out of my office, I could see it on your face. You're happy, and you deserve it, Hae! Seriously, you do. I know you haven't told me everything that's happened between you and that asshole ex of yours, but I know you enough to know you're a good person and friend. You're an amazing mom to Huxie!"

She reaches her arms out, and I stand. Wrapping my arms around her in a hug, I whisper a muffled, "Thank you," in her ear.

My phone vibrates on my desk. Madelyn doesn't mind if I keep my phone on in case my mom or the school reach out about Huxton.

We break apart, and I reach for my phone, checking and finding Corbin's name on the screen. A slow smile spreads across my face when I see it's him.

"I texted him a link to the Facebook post this morning, and he replied he was only a good model because of you." She grins playfully, swatting my arm.

I purse my lips and shake my head. "Of course, he did."

"I've never seen him like this. To be honest, he's lived the bachelor life since Alex first introduced us. He's like a changed man now. Even the rest of the world is falling in love with the two of you together."

I swipe the screen to open the message.

Corbin: Mornin', beautiful. It looks like we've caught the attention of the internet, and they seem to agree. I can never keep my hands off you when I'm around you.

I blush.

"What'd he say?"

"Nothin'…" I trail off. "He's a smooth talker, and that's what worries me. There's not a single thing wrong with him. Nothing that has me concerned or second-guessing everything. Aside from it being too soon. Something has to be wrong with this man. He has to have some skeleton hiding in his closet."

Madelyn chuckles, looking from side to side, then shrugs. "I don't think there is, Hae. If there was, I haven't heard a thing about it."

"It's like I'm waiting for the other shoe to drop or that I'll end up letting my own fears and insecurities get in the way somehow, and it'll ruin everything."

"You can't let it, though. If you let your mind create all these scenarios in your head of what could go wrong, you'll never get a chance to truly see what it could be. Sometimes you just have to take a leap of faith and trust where you land."

"Yeah, I've done that before, and now look where I am."

"Listen, I know I don't know everything that happened between you and Atlas, but I know enough. It's not fair to you or to Corbin to compare him to your ex."

She's right. Although there were a lot of red flags I over-looked. I chose to believe what he told me rather than listen to my intuition.

I don't get those feelings when I'm around Corbin, though. Nothing in my mind or in my gut warns me to tread lightly.

Maybe she's right. Maybe I just need to trust him and see where it goes.

Madelyn leaves me to get logged in for the day, warning me I'll have a lot to get caught up on.

I hadn't even been online or checked in on things. Corbin scooted out the door before Huxton woke up. I didn't want him to find Corbin in my bed and ask questions I wasn't prepared to answer. I was pleasantly surprised when I had an unexpected breakfast delivery arrive.

Corbin ended up leaving, running home to clean up and stopping back with breakfast from Oh My Goodies. He didn't stay long, sneaking in a kiss before saying he had to stop by his parents' house.

After a long night of lovemaking, we curled up in bed with nothing between us, and he opened up about why he decided to go into law enforcement.

He shared with me about his family background and how his mom had also moved to Arbor Creek with the hopes of a fresh start. Although our circumstances were vastly different, I couldn't help but recognize how similar our paths were. We both knew what it was like to be betrayed by the people we loved. I admired her courage after all she'd gone through.

The way he described her as this strong and nurturing woman explained so much about why he is the way he is, especially in how he treats me and Huxton.

The rest of the day and into the afternoon flew by uneventfully. I was slammed with emails and messages, but I wasn't complaining in the least because it kept me busy.

Madelyn came up for air around lunchtime, and we ate together before she took off back to her office to continue editing her photos.

It's after four thirty when I finally shut down my computer. My mom is meeting me at the house to drop off Huxton. She's been helping me pick him up after school. I usually will stop by her house on the way home, but tonight was a bit different from our routine since Atlas asked to switch his night with Huxton to tonight, leaving me with little time.

I didn't want to bother Madelyn on my way out, knowing how stressed she's been these past few days. When we talked over lunch, I offered to take more off her plate, but she assured me I was doing enough by keeping a handle on her social media and schedule.

Corbin planned on stopping over for dinner, giving us a chance to spend time alone while Huxton was with his dad.

I step outside, locking up behind me while Madelyn was hiding in her office. I didn't want anyone showing up unannounced.

"Haelynn?" The voice coming from behind me catches me off guard. I spin on my heels, nearly falling against the side of the building.

My eyes land on Gage.

"Gage, hey. I'm sorry, I didn't even see or hear you coming."

"I'm sorry. Did I scare you? I wasn't trying to." He feigns innocence, shrugging his shoulders. The condescending nature of his tone throws me off.

"It's okay…" I try to assure him and myself in the process. Something about this conversation isn't sitting well with me.

"It's Haelynn, right? Is that what scared you? Me calling you by your name?"

"No?" I question. "I didn't hear you. Do you often sneak up on women?"

He steps back, holding his hands up, and shakes his head.

"Listen, I'm not trying to freak you out, so I'm sorry if I did." This time, he sounds sincere, so I force myself to let it go. If Corbin trusts him, I should too.

"I have a question for you, and I'm hoping you can help clear this up, and we can put it to rest. What do you know about me and my family?"

"Excuse me?"

"You had to have recognized my name, right? Gage Shaw… did that not raise any questions for you when Corbin introduced us?"

"I'm sorry, I'm not following," I say, my brows furrow, looking around trying to piece this together.

"Your father is Marc Krate, right? Were you ever going to tell Corbin, or did that not seem like an important piece of detail to share when you showed up here?"

Truth be told, I never had the chance to meet my father. My mom wouldn't say much about him growing up, only that he wasn't a good man before he died.

For the longest time, I thought it was hard to speak about him because the pain of losing him still ran deep.

"I don't know what you're talking about. Mention what? What did my father do?"

"He's the reason my uncle is dead." Gage grunts. "I don't know what your intentions are with Corbin either, but the last thing our families need is you taking anything more from us. You hear me? So just stay away from me and from him, stay away from us all."

My heart drops in the pit of my stomach, replaying him saying my father is the reason his uncle is gone. I want to stop him and beg him to explain, but before I have a chance, he brushes past me and storms off toward his pickup. He slams the door shut behind him and speeds off down the road.

All this time, I've waited for the other shoe to drop, for some warning sign I need to stay away from Corbin.

Anything.

It turns out he was the one who needed a warning.

chapter fifteen

HAELYNN

My mind is in disarray. I don't even know how I manage to make it back to my place without ending up in an accident.

One second, I'm climbing in the car, and the next, I'm pulling into the driveway without any recollection of driving home. My mom is parked along the street. I'm thankful she doesn't stick around. I have a ton of questions for her, questions only she'd have the answers to, but I can't seem to wrap my mind around everything right now. I don't want to have this conversation in front of Huxton either.

He climbs out of his booster seat as I open the door, taking off running toward the house.

"Hey, sweetie." She smiles, turning to look at me from where I stand near the back passenger side. "You okay?"

"Yeah, just a crazy day is all." I rub my fingers over my forehead, attempting to massage the skin from where the dull headache is starting to form.

"You have the night to yourself. Try to enjoy it, relax a bit."

She doesn't know about Corbin or that I've been seeing anyone. I can imagine what she'd think and say if she knew. That's a conversation for another day.

"Have a good night." I force a smile, tossing her a wave over my shoulder.

I'm no more than two steps in the door when I glance at the clock, noticing the time reads nine minutes until five. Atlas will be here soon, and knowing Corbin will be here shortly thereafter is the only thing pushing me forward.

Huxton sits at the table with his book bag in front of him, pulling out papers and books he must've checked out today. I'm about to ask him how his day was when two hard knocks deflate all the energy out of me.

Huxton's eyes dart up to mine, and I notice the uneasy smile on his face. He doesn't say it, and he would never tell his dad this, but I know he doesn't want to go with him any more than I would.

I hate even more that I can't be there with him, not knowing what's going on while he's gone.

"It's a short visit tonight. You'll be home after eight."

He nods, shoving his stuff back into his bag as I turn and amble toward the door.

The sun shines brightly through the screen door, and he's dressed in a dark-gray dress shirt and black slacks. His hair is styled neatly with a dark pair of aviators covering his eyes.

He's handsome, and God, doesn't he know it. If I didn't know him the way I do, he'd be a total package in the looks department.

It's too bad he's rotting from the inside out.

My lip curls, and I mentally tell myself not to let him see the disgust on my face.

He reaches for the door handle and lets himself inside. I grit my teeth in annoyance, stopping in my tracks as he lets the screen door slam shut behind him.

One thing I've learned after talking with my therapist is when you've been abused, you notice little things about people. You study their body language more than most people, especially your abuser. You can sense when they're tense, when they may be angry, and you try to keep yourself five steps ahead of them, never wanting to be caught off guard.

Maybe my interaction with Gage earlier has me on high alert, or maybe just being around Atlas puts me on edge, but anxiety coils in my stomach like a venomous snake ready to attack.

He reaches his hand up, pulling his glasses away from his face, and I know the moment he does, he's drunk. His eyes are red and bloodshot.

If he thinks for a second I'm about to let Huxton leave with him, he's out of his damn mind.

"Have you been drinking?"

"Huxton, can you go to your room, please?" he says it as a question, but the authority rings clear in his voice. It's not meant as a question, but a command.

Huxton nods, ducking his head so his chin touches his chest. He rounds the dining room table, turning to walk toward his room when he stops and glances over at me.

"Mom...?" he says.

"It's okay, sweetie. You can take my phone with you and play your game while I talk to your dad. It's in my purse. Okay?"

He nods, swiping my phone from the table. He looks back over at me, dipping his head back down, and stalks down the hall.

Once I hear the click of Huxton's door closing, my head darts back to Atlas. Anger simmers in my blood.

"You can't possibly think I'd let him go with you when you've been drinking, Atlas. Are you out of your damn mind? Why would you even drive here? Don't you know what could happen if you got into an accident?"

"When were you going to tell me you've been seeing that guy from the other night?"

My heart thumps wildly in my chest, thoughts swirling through my mind.

"Wha-what? What are you talking about? What guy?"

"Don't play stupid with me, Haelynn." He takes a step toward me.

I'm still turned from when I was talking to Huxton, so the move forces my back against the wall. He towers over me.

"Atlas, please don't do this. You're drunk."

"Don't do what, Haelynn? You're the one who left me, took my son, and decided to move into this piece of shit house. Now come to find out, you're fuckin' some guy behind my back. Have you forgotten you're still married? That means you're mine as long as our marriage is still legal."

He tilts his head down, tracing his nose along the side of my jaw.

"You're fuckin' mine, and I think you need to be reminded of that fact. Don't you?" Spit shoots out of his mouth, hitting the side of my face.

He reaches his hand up, grabbing my arm. It's still tender from the last time, causing me to wince.

"No." I grit my teeth, attempting to jerk my arm away from him. "I'm not yours. As far as I'm concerned, I haven't been yours since the first time you put your hands on me."

"Excuse me?" He slams my arm against the wall above my head. "I don't know who you think you are, but I think you've forgotten who you're speaking to."

"Atlas, let me go right now. Let me go and leave or I'm going to call the cops."

"Oh really? You going to call that little fucking punk of yours to come over here? Is that what you're going to do?"

How does he know who Corbin is and where he works?

He grins, and it turns into a laugh. Maniacal. It sends a chill down my spine.

"What? You didn't think I knew? Did you think I hadn't heard after pictures of the two of you are splattered all over the fuckin' internet?"

I sigh in defeat.

"Did you think I wasn't going to see them? Like the word wasn't going to get around? I got people in my fucking office coming up to me, asking about pictures of *my wife* with another man. I have to find out from one of the guys at work."

He finally releases my arm, letting it drop to my side. He doesn't move, keeping me pinned against the wall. The familiar pain shoots up my arm.

"Atlas, it's not how it looks, but it doesn't matter. We're separated, and we're getting a divorce. Although it's not finalized yet, what I do now is none of your concern."

"None of my concern? Are you kidding me? I told you I'm not letting you go. I'm not signing those fucking papers. When you married me, it was for better or for worse."

"You don't get to pick which vows mean something and which ones don't. I'm not having this argument with you. You need to leave."

Two knocks interrupt us, sending Atlas's gaze shooting toward the door.

"You've got to be fuckin' kidding me," he growls under his breath. "The motherfucker shows up here with my son down the hall."

He pushes himself back, crossing the distance from where we're standing to the door. "What can I do for you, officer?"

"Ahh, is Haelynn here?" Corbin asks, attempting to peer over Atlas's shoulder. Atlas rests his forearm against the doorframe, making it harder to see past him.

"Yes, she is. She's my wife. We're about to sit down and eat dinner," he lies. He's playing it off like he has no idea about the two of us, attempting to throw Corbin off by his response.

"We had a call come in, someone concerned about yelling coming from over here. Small town, you know. People get worried. Can I speak to her myself? I just need to check and make sure everything is all right."

"Phone call? From who?" Atlas looks out the window, searching for any sign of a nosy neighbor who may be outside overhearing our conversation.

Huxton.

"That information is not pertinent at the moment, sir. I'm going to have to ask you to step outside."

I spot another officer behind Corbin and suck in a deep breath. He signals with his fingers for Atlas to come outside. He pushes the screen door open, stepping out onto the porch and jogging down the front stoop.

I turn to go down the hall to check on Huxton. Tears prick my eyes, and my heart aches at the thought of him making the phone call.

"Sir, if you don't calm down, I'll have to put you in cuffs."

I rush toward the door, seeing Atlas and Corbin standing toe-to-toe.

"What? You didn't think I knew you were trying to move in on my wife?"

He shakes his head. I'm not sure if he's trying to cover up a laugh or resisting the urge to put him in his place. Corbin's partner forces his arm between the two of them, attempting to separate him, but it doesn't stop Atlas. He's like a rabid dog. He doesn't back down.

In one quick move, I watch as Atlas shoves his partner to the side while simultaneously spitting in Corbin's face. It's a cheap shot, catching him off guard right before he lands a punch in his face.

I scream at Atlas to stop. Corbin shakes it off, clenching his jaw before he lowers his shoulder and tackles Atlas to the ground.

"Don't fucking move!" his partner shouts.

Corbin uses the sleeve of his uniform to wipe the spit off his face, moving his jaw from side to side. He peers up, noticing me standing in the doorway. Once they get the cuffs on him, he pushes off him and heads toward me.

I open the screen door to let him in and move into the living room to avoid anyone, especially Atlas, from seeing us.

"Are you okay?" he asks when he turns the corner, and I don't hesitate to wrap my arms around his neck, needing him. His arms circle my waist, pulling me toward him.

"I'm so sorry." My words are muffled through tears, my face pressed against the side of his face, inhaling his clean scent mixed with sweat.

"You're sorry? You have nothing to be sorry for, Hae. Nothing."

"I'm just sorry you have to deal with this, with me and all my baggage."

"Stop, don't even say that."

He reaches his hand up, running it over my hair. His soothing helps ease the flood of emotions rushing through me.

We don't move, standing in the living room for a few moments. I tilt my head back and wipe tears from my eyes.

"I should go check on Huxton."

Corbin nods. "He's the one who called."

"I figured he was." The confirmation sends another stream of tears flooding down my face. The guilt of the situation ate me up inside.

I feel like an awful parent for bringing him into the world with such a toxic relationship with his father, and now I've made it worse by getting involved with another man.

Not even a day has passed since I said it, and just like I expected, everything has come crashing down around me. It's not even Corbin to blame either.

"We'll have to get your statement and take him in. You can go check on Huxton. I'll stop by after he goes to bed to check in."

All I want right now is to be with Huxton. He's the one who needs me right now. Everything else will have to wait.

He squeezes my hand when I step back, walking down the hall toward Huxton's room. I release a heavy sigh, attempting to shake myself from the thoughts plaguing me. When I push the door open, I find Huxton on the floor in his beanbag chair, his headphones on while he stares at my phone.

His eyes dart up to mine, flashing me a hesitant smile.

"Are you okay, sweetie?"

He nods. "Is Corbin here? I heard yelling, and I called him. He said if we ever need him to give him a call, and he'd get here lightning fast. He told me to stay in my room and put on my headphones until one of you came to get me."

My lip trembles. "He's here. Everything is okay. I'm sorry you had to hear yelling."

Huxton pushes himself up from his spot on the floor and crosses the room toward me. I bend down on the floor in front of him, wrapping him in a tight hug.

"I'm sorry, sweetie."

My chest aches. It seems like no matter how hard I try, I can't escape my broken life. It's all I want for him, for us.

"It's all right." His words are muffled against the side of my neck. "I hate when Dad makes you sad."

I don't even know how to respond to him. I hate the thought of him seeing what this does to me, burdening him with things he shouldn't have to deal with at his age.

"Let's do something fun tonight, just the two of us. We could make a picnic basket and go to the park to eat dinner. How's that sound?"

He pulls back, his eyes lighting up as he nods enthusiastically.

"Perfect." I grin. "Spending the time with my favorite boy always makes me happy."

He goes back to playing his game, and I step out into the hallway, needing a moment to myself. Walking into the bathroom, I shut the door behind me. As I lean against the closed door, the cold wood soothes my heated skin as I slide down to sit on the floor.

I run the palm of my hands over my face. I don't bother to hold back the tears as my silent cries wrack through my body.

My head is a mess, and my heart is heavy with the weight of today bearing down on me.

It will get better. One day, it will all get better.

I can't lose hope that the day would come when we'd break free. For me, for Huxton.

chapter sixteen

CORBIN

It's been two days since I've seen or heard from Haelynn. After the incident with Atlas at her place, I decided to move forward with pressing charges. He's managed to avoid any marks on his record for years after mistreating Haelynn. He's used his money and power to intimidate her before, but it won't work this time.

If he's capable of putting his hands on a police officer, there's no doubt in my mind he was capable of worse.

I don't want to push her to talk to me, so I try to stay busy to distract myself, but it was difficult when she wasn't responding to my texts. I skipped my morning coffee dates with Layla and have been hitting up the gym more often. The anger and frustration I've felt weigh on me, and it was the only way for me to release some steam.

When my shift is over for the day, I considered going back home to unwind. I decided against it, not wanting more time to think about everything. I opted to go for a run instead.

By the time I finished, I was ready to eat dinner and crash.

The next day, I woke up early to head to Everton. I've been teaching a traffic enforcement course as a part of the Police Academy training. I was in desperate need of a change of pace, and this gave me the distraction I was looking for to get my mind off Haelynn.

What I hadn't considered was how word had gotten out and people recognized me, asking a million questions about the photos Madelyn shared online.

I pulled my truck up later that night outside Brodie's and put it in park. Alex texted me, asking if I wanted to meet up with him and Gage for dinner and to grab a beer. I wasn't in the mood to drink, but with nothing else to fill my time, I opted to take them up on the offer.

My eyes immediately were drawn to the bench outside the bar, facing the street running through downtown, recalling the last time I was here and how Haelynn had sat there waiting for me.

I wish I could go back to that night, wanting to relive our time together. Back to the night of the bonfire when we snuck over to her place for time alone, just the two of us. Better yet, back to the night I made love to her, and we fell asleep with her in my arms.

I called Madelyn yesterday to check in on how Haelynn was doing. She urged me to be patient, reminding me of what brought her to Arbor Creek. Although she knew I had good intentions and was good for her, Haelynn wasn't searching for a relationship when I walked into the studio and her life that day.

It was a hard realization to accept, but Madelyn had a point. Maybe she isn't ready for a relationship. I fear if I push her too hard, she'll take off running, and I'll lose her altogether.

If she needs time and space, I'll do my best to give her what she wants. I just don't want to lose her for good.

I spot Gage's pickup just as Alex pulls into the spot next to me. He greets me with a brief nod. I push my door open, hollering, "What's up!" as I slam the door shut behind me.

"How you hangin' in there, man?"

I know by the tone and the way he raises his brow, he's referring to the incident over at Haelynn's. I returned after she put Huxton to bed, allowing her to calm down before taking her statement. Alex stopped me as I was leaving to see how I was doing. He could tell there was a lot on my mind, so he dropped it.

"I'm all right. I'd be doing a helluva lot better if she'd talk to me, but I'm giving her time."

He nods. "Madelyn mentioned she's been working from home the past couple of days. They're so damn busy now after posting those pictures of you two all over the internet. You see all those people talking about you and your ugly mug?"

Alex elbows me jokingly. He jogs ahead toward the door to grab the handle, stepping back to let me through.

We spot Gage at one of the high-top tables across the bar. A solemn expression marks his features. His elbows rest on the table with a bottle of beer in his hand, studying the label, seemingly lost in thought.

"I had to turn off notifications on the post because my phone started going haywire. I couldn't keep up with them all."

I knew the photos would be a hit, but I hadn't expected the response. I couldn't help but wonder how Haelynn felt about it.

I claim a seat on the barstool across from Gage, and Alex takes the one on the right. The server approaches as soon as we sit down, ready to take our orders. We've been here enough to know we don't need to look at the menu to know what we want.

Alex talks about some work he hoped to start before the fall weather hit us, wanting to take advantage of the few warm days we had left. It's easy, and I'm grateful they invited me out, knowing how much I needed this right now.

"How have things been over at Compass?" I ask.

Gage was quiet for most of dinner. Something that's been happening all too often lately. Things have been off between us since the day I dropped by on my lunch break. Tensions have only been building since the way he spoke to Haelynn at the bonfire.

I know Gage comes from a good place. We've been best friends since we were little, and our parents have been close our entire lives. We used to tell each other everything, but lately, something's been bothering him, and I have yet to get to the bottom of it.

"Same ole," he mutters under his breath, lifting the bottle to his lips to take a swig.

Alex raises his brows, shaking his head. He's just as baffled by his attitude as I am.

"What's your deal lately? You've been different these past few weeks. Agitated and on edge."

He glances at me and then back to Alex. I want to tell him to cut the bullshit.

"Did I do something? What the hell has gotten into you?"

"What's gotten into me?" He slams his empty bottle down on the table. "You're quick to want to talk about what's gotten into me. How about what's goin' on with you?" He scoffs.

"You're gonna have to clue me in because I have no idea what you're getting at here. Clearly, you're pissed about something, so spit it out already."

"Spit it out. He wants me to spit it out." He chuckles, shaking his head. "Well, how about we start from the beginning? Why don't we start with how you've been seeing Haelynn? Are you going to sit here and pretend it's not supposed to bother me?"

My mouth drops open, gaping at him. I rub my hand over my jaw, confused. For a second, I question whether they know each other or have some history, but it doesn't make sense.

I know Haelynn wouldn't lie to me. Certainly, that's not what has him so upset.

"What the hell are you talking about? Bother *you*? Why would my relationship with her bother you?"

He sneers. "Oh, so Marc Krate's daughter mysteriously drops into town, and I'm supposed to be okay with my best friend going off and hooking up with her?"

The name Marc Krate rings clear through my mind. It's not a name that would be relevant to most people, but our jobs and our families' history with the Krates are no secret to us.

This is far more personal for Gage than I ever realized.

Marc Krate is the reason Gage, his namesake, is dead. He's the reason he is who he is today, sitting right before me.

I have no words, staring at him with my jaw slack, unable to form a response to argue with him other than I had no idea. He can't think for a second I had any inkling who her father was.

"Shit," Alex mutters under his breath.

It's like someone handed me a live grenade, and with a pull of the pin, everything in my world just blew up around me.

chapter seventeen

HAELYNN

Madelyn didn't bat an eye when I asked if I could finish out the week working from home. I was still trying to wrap my head around everything that happened, and being home felt like the best place to do so.

My number one priority right now is focusing on Huxton, but I can't forget my conversation with Gage outside the studio.

He warned me to stay away from him and his friends. Although I know he was mostly talking about Corbin, Madelyn was lumped into it too. I get he was looking out for his friends, but I still can't understand why he felt he needed to protect them from me of all people.

The way he looked at me, as if I was some sort of toxic imprint on their lives, and the only way to fix it would be to stay away from them.

I hadn't planned on doing this, but when my mom called asking to take Huxton for the night, I jumped on it. It gave me the night to myself. Something that didn't happen often these days.

I made the quick drive to her place with my windows down. The moisture in the air was thick. The news said there's a big storm rolling through the Midwest. The sky was already beginning to turn a mixture of midnight blue and dark purple. It's an ominous feeling, much like how I'm anticipating the rest of the night going.

I push the thought out of my mind when I pull into my mom's driveway. She must've been waiting at the door because she pushes it open to greet us as soon as she sees us. Her hair is pulled up on top of her head, and her robe is tied around her waist.

I fully expected to walk in and find her on the couch, *Wheel of Fortune* playing on the TV, with her candles lit around the house.

"There's my sweet boy." She grins. Huxton takes off past me, racing toward the door.

"Hey, Huxie, can you do me a favor and play in the toy room for a bit? I need to talk to Gram for a minute."

My mom's eyes narrow at me. She must sense the change in my demeanor. I haven't been able to get this conversation off my mind since my run-in with Gage.

For all my life, I believed what my mom told me about my biological father. I sat and stewed on this forever last night after I put Huxton to bed, but bits and pieces from my memory still weren't adding up.

I vaguely recall being about Huxton's age the first time she brought me back to Iowa. I've never forgotten because it was the first and only time I've visited a prison. At the time, I had no reason to think any differently. She told me we were seeing a friend of hers, but there's something about the trip I couldn't forget.

I remember the tears in his eyes and the look on his face when she introduced me to him. He had a tattoo near his temple, but his smile was a mixture of pride and sadness.

Toward the end of our visit, I could sense the change in her demeanor. I've only seen her this upset a few times, all of them for a good reason, except for this day. I don't know what spurred it, but it was like a switch was flipped, and she was ready to leave.

She pushed me to stand behind her, hoping I wouldn't overhear the words she uttered next. Thinking back on them now, I can still hear them run through my mind the same way she spoke them that day.

"You will never see or hear from her again. As far as I'm concerned, you're dead to me. You're dead to both of us."

She never spoke of him or that day again. I never put two and two together, believing the lies she had told me about him passing away in an accident before I was born.

The first two weeks after she told me, I mourned the loss of the man I never knew. I cried over the father I never got the chance to meet and all the important milestones in life he'd miss out on.

I asked her once if she'd take me to visit his grave, and she promised me one day she'd take me there, but that day never came.

Staring back at her now, I recognize the disappointment shrouding her eyes. Her shoulders slouch forward, resigning to the defeat she's fought against for too long.

All this time, she's been feeding me a lie. She knows what's coming, and it's time she tells me the truth.

Huxton stares up at me, nodding his head before he wraps his arms around my waist.

"Don't worry, sweetie. I'll come say bye to you before I leave. We just need a couple of minutes. Okay?"

He nods before taking off toward his playroom. Chipper, my mom's puppy, barrels down the hall after him. Only the sound of his paws on the floor mixed with Huxton's left behind.

"I guess we should probably sit down for this, huh?"

I drop Huxton's overnight bag by the door and toe off my shoes.

I wasn't planning on staying long, but I wanted the truth, and then I needed time away to reconcile it all.

She lets out a heavy sigh as she takes a seat in her recliner, and I follow, choosing to sit across from her on the couch. She picks up the remote and turns off the television, her eyes staring at the worn carpet.

My heart thumps wildly. I can practically hear the pounding in my ears.

"Haelynn, you should know everything I've ever done was to protect you, to keep you safe. I'm not perfect. I've made my fair share of mistakes, but it was always to protect you."

I nodded. Whatever reasons she had for keeping the truth from me, I knew I had to put myself in her shoes and consider why she did it. There's nothing I wouldn't do for Huxton to keep him safe. It's the very reason I got us out when I did.

We sat there in silence for God knows how long. I almost wonder if she's not sure how to break the ice and come out and tell me, so I do us both the favor and cut to the chase.

"Is my father... is his name Marc Krate?"

She squeezes her eyes shut and lets out a heavy exhale. "Yes."

My heart clenches in my chest. I've read so much about this man since Gage confronted me. I wanted to know everything about him and understand who he was before I came here.

"Is it true?" I ask, glancing up at her. "Did he do what they say he did?"

She nods again, a tear leaking from her eye and streaming down her cheek.

"Your father, when we first met, was a sweet and loving man. He would've given up anything for me. In a way, he did. He got mixed up with the wrong crowd. His cousin too. It didn't take me long to figure out he was using drugs. When I gave him an ultimatum, forcing him to choose between me or that life, he did what I had hoped he would."

You could hear the hurt in her words. It made my heart ache for her.

"He told me everything I wanted to hear. He made promise after promise to walk away from that life, to get sober and be a better man."

I knew what it was like to be on the receiving end of those empty promises and to hope they'll follow through with them.

"Things were good for a short time until they weren't. He started disappearing. I'd call him, and his phone would be turned off. He'd be gone for days at a time. This was right before I found out I was pregnant with you."

"I heard about the accident on the news. I grew up with Gage Shaw. We went to the same school. I was in the same grade as his cousin Graham. They were good people. Hardworking."

"It was all over the news when it happened. Everyone knew the make and model of the car they believed ran Gage off the road. His car flipped several times before landing upside down, killing him instantly. It was a similar car to the one your uncle Isaac drove. He didn't get it out often. It was an old classic. When I confronted your dad, he lost it. He called me every name in the book and told me whoever filled my head full of lies would pay for it."

Her chin trembles. She cups her hand over her mouth, tears filling her eyes before the dam breaks, and they flow freely down her face.

I want to go to her and hold her. When I attempt to move, she holds her hand up and releases a deep breath.

"I'm okay. I'll be fine. I just need to get through this."

She reaches for a tissue off the end table and dabs it under her eyes.

"When I found out I was pregnant with you, things only worsened. I couldn't trust him, and I sure as hell wasn't going to trust him to take care of you. I was terrified of the people he was running around with. They were bad people, and I had a feeling it was the reason Gage was gone. I didn't want you to grow up in this life. I wanted better for you. When I saw the opportunity to get out, I ran like hell out of Arbor Creek and didn't look back."

I can practically see the weight of the secret lift off her shoulders. She slumps back against her chair, her hands shaking as she runs the tissue underneath her eyes.

She takes a deep breath. When she finally looks up and meets my gaze, a small smile curves the edge of her mouth.

"I'm sorry, Hae. I'm so very sorry."

My heart aches at the sight of her like this. I know without a doubt she was doing what she felt was best for me. Knowing he's in prison now solidifies it.

"You have nothing to be sorry for, Mom. I will never be sorry for walking away from Atlas because I know it was best for me and Huxton."

She chokes out a sob, covering her mouth again as she nods. This time, I give in and go to her, kneeling on the floor in front of her as she leans forward to wrap her arms around me in a hug.

"I should've told you sooner. You deserved..." Her voice cracks. "You deserved to know the truth, and I'm sorry it took me so long to gather the courage to be honest."

"It's okay."

I pull back and brush my thumb under her eyes, wiping the tears away.

"When you were born, I gave you my last name. Not many people know the truth. The last time I spoke to your father, I made him promise me to keep it that way. He agreed, only because he knew I was right. When he got put away, he brought a large drug operation down with him. I didn't want them to try to hurt him by coming after us. It took years before I felt safe enough to come back here, but Arbor Creek is my home."

I move to the edge of the chair and wrap my arms around her. Huxton eventually emerges from his toy room, poking his little head around the corner.

"I think it's been more than a couple of minutes, Mom. Can I come out now?"

I chuckled. "Of course, honey. C'mere."

I wave him over, and he crawls up with us, sprawling his legs out across our laps.

"I'm going to take off and let you and Gram spend some time together."

I kneel in front of Huxton and wrap his small body in a hug.

"I'll be by tomorrow morning to pick him up. Maybe we can all go get breakfast. Ooh, or some chocolate pancakes. I know this great place downtown we can check out. You in?"

Huxton's eyes light up, and he nods his head enthusiastically.

"Count me in!" He gives me two thumbs-up as a crooked grin stretches across his face.

My mom's gaze burns into me. I know how much regret she feels right now, and I hate how much it bothers her.

"It's okay, Mom. Please don't beat yourself up over this."

I pull her in for a hug, running my hand over her back.

"Some decisions come with sacrifices, but we can't be sorry for protecting the people we love."

Her sad smile returns, and she nods, peering down at Huxton from where he sits on the floor in front of us, playing with his Hot Wheels.

"Some sacrifices are worth it all."

chapter eighteen

HAELYNN

As I climb back in my car, my phone dings with a text alert. I hadn't thought ahead about what I wanted to do with the night to myself. It's been a long week, and I could use some "me" time.

When I see Corbin's name on my screen, my heart sinks into the pit of my stomach.

He's tried to reach out to me all week, but his messages were met with no response. If I'm being honest, I didn't know what to say to him. After my conversation with my mom, I still had so many thoughts swirling through my mind. I could barely wrap my head around how I'd begin to explain it to him.

Corbin: Please talk to me.

As soon as he sees I've read his message, another text dings.

Corbin: Haelynn... please.

He doesn't deserve for me to keep pushing him off, and knowing that's what I'm doing makes me feel even worse. He deserves to know why our relationship can't go any further. I just don't know if I have the strength to break it to him yet.

It wasn't fair of me to put him through this, though. I didn't want to hurt him or myself more than I have, especially when he's been so good to me and Huxton.

Me: Can I come see you?

He responds right away with a "yes" followed by his address. I have an idea of where he lives after he mentioned living in one of the farmhouses along the main road leading out of Arbor Creek. There weren't too many other houses it could be.

It took me less than five minutes to drive from my mom's house to his place. On one hand, I could've used more time, but I knew this had to be done one way or another. Avoiding it wouldn't change the reality of the situation.

It's early September, and the leaves have begun to change. The sky continues to grow darker by the minute as the daylight dwindles. The wind whips through the trees lining the property, a clear sign that the storm brewing will be wicked.

I pull my car into the driveway, parking in the open spot next to Corbin's pickup. A large garage sits on the backside of the property. You wouldn't see it if you were driving past, but something about seeing his truck makes me feel closer to him, knowing he wasn't too far away.

It's a beautifully crafted farmhouse with a wraparound porch. The swing on the front, just below the second-story balcony, gave all the small-town farm life feels. Immediately, my mind drifts off to thoughts of Huxton growing up here, playing in the yard and swinging with me on a warm spring day. My heart aches with dread at the thought of losing the future with Corbin I can so clearly see.

The paint on the old house is chipping, the wood worn and distressed over the years. When I round the back of my car to climb the steps, the deep timbre of his voice has me stopping in my tracks.

"Hey," he says, sending chills through me.

I turn to look at him from where he stands. He's holding a dirty rag, wiping off the dirt or oil marking his hands covering the front of his pants.

He's wearing a long sleeve plaid button-up shirt with the top few buttons undone, showing his tan skin beneath the material. My eyes drop to the hint of chest hair, biting down on my lip before my gaze finds his.

Once again, my own thoughts reign terror on me as I picture him stalking in through the door as I'm making dinner after he's been outside working in the yard. My mind filters back to how sexy he looked standing in my kitchen the night he stayed over, memories of him shirtless leaning over the top of me.

"This is a pleasant surprise. I started to wonder if I'd ever see or talk to you again."

Seeing him now, I don't know if I'll be able to work up the courage to walk away from him. I hate the thought of him looking at me differently than he does now, knowing once I break down and tell him the truth, it will change how he sees me forever.

A part of me wished I could push all the thoughts and fears piling up in my mind and soak up this feeling with him for a little longer. I know how selfish it would be of me to do, though.

He shoves the rag into his pocket and crosses the driveway toward me. I suck in a quick breath, twisting my fingers in my hands. The urge to reach out and touch him is making it impossible right now.

His gaze drops to my hands, bouncing back to where my bottom lip is caught between my teeth. A smile lines the edge of his mouth, and he knows he's got me.

"We have so much we need to talk about…" My voice trails off.

He flicks his thumb over his chin, nodding before looking back at me. Sweat dots his brow, and he raises his forearm to dab it off.

"We do."

He takes a step toward me. The closer we get to each other, the more intoxicated I feel.

"Corbin," I mutter, staring at him when he stops a foot away from me.

He reaches his hand out and grips my hip, pulling me closer to him. My hands press against his firm chest, running over his pecs, feeling every delicious ridge of his body.

"Mm-hmm," he hums, leaning his head closer to me.

His cologne mixed with the scent of his sweat sends my heart into a tailspin.

Lightning flashes behind him in the distance, but I'm incapable of taking my eyes off him.

"When I'm around you..." I exhale harshly. "It's like nothing else exists outside of the two of us."

Thunder follows, rumbling in the distance, growing closer to us this time.

I tilt my head back to peer up at him beneath my lashes. His eyes drop to my lips, and he subtly bites his own as if anticipating what I'm going to say next.

"I need you to help me forget everything right now."

His breath feathers across my lips, pulling me closer to him. His nearness makes my senses spin.

"I'll be whatever you need," he vows.

He reaches his hands down, gripping my thighs to lift me into his arms. My legs circle his waist.

The rain beats down around us, hitting my face and wetting my hair. Neither of us stops; his tongue brushes across my lips, seeking entry.

"Corbin," I groan, holding his face in my hands and opening my mouth to him. He presses his forehead against mine, releasing a strangled breath.

"God, I've missed you. I've missed this."

He's careful of his movements as he hurries up the steps, his grip on my thighs never waning. He reaches for the door handle, sending it slamming against the side of the house before springing shut behind us. We barely make it more than two steps inside before he has my back pressed against the wall.

"I need to feel you. Taste you. Every inch of your body."

He helps me to my feet, but my legs feel like jelly under the haze of desire. I reach for the buttons on his shirt, attempting to quickly undo them before he bats my hand away and rips his shirt open. My jaw drops at the sound of the buttons hitting the hardwood floors.

"I can't wait any longer."

A smug smile spreads across his face. I lift the hem of my shirt over my head, tossing it on the floor next to us. He shrugs off his shirt, adding it to the pile before lifting me back into his arms. The coolness from the wall against my heated skin causes goose bumps to break across my body.

"Haelynn," he moans, nipping and sucking along my shoulder toward my neck.

"Stay with me," he mutters, the pain in his voice hitting me once again. "Promise me you'll stay with me."

I don't know what to say, and I'm scared my honesty will pull us from the moment. I'm not ready to have this conversation yet. If this is the last night I'll have with him, if it's the last memory we'll have together, I want to savor every second.

"I'm not going anywhere," I whisper against his lips, clutching his face in my hands. "There's nowhere else I want to be."

He sucks in a breath and squeezes his eyes shut, landing a kiss on my mouth. This time, it's slow and full of passion. Each move is deliberate as if he's trying to tell me something with his body.

I'm waiting for the moment when one of us makes the move and says what we're both feeling out loud, but the thought scares me.

He grips my hips, wrapping his arm around my lower back, and carries me down the hallway. The farther we get into the house, the darker it is. But he leads the way, and I trust him.

The storm outside these four walls rages on like the one wreaking havoc on my mind, but I do my best to push it away.

He carries me into the bedroom. I spot the king-sized bed centered among the large bay windows with a small light near the corner, leading to what looks like a bathroom.

He sets me down on the edge of the bed, kissing me once again. My fingers reach out toward him, brushing against his belt. He dips his head to my shoulder, his breath coming out in heavy pants while I expertly try to unhook the buckle. He straightens, moving between my legs.

I gaze up at him beneath my eyelashes, unzipping his pants, then slipping my fingers into the front of his boxer briefs.

He sucks in a breath once again and squeezes his eyes shut when my fingers brush against his silky skin, gripping him in my fist.

"Dear God," he chokes out.

I pump my hand over him, and his eyes find mine burning into me. His chest heaves with each heavy breath, raking his teeth over his lower lip.

A bead of precum leaks from the tip. I pump him long and slow, relishing the way his body reacts to me. The changes in his breathing and the small groans he makes each time I brush my fingers over the sensitive head turn me on more.

He wraps his hand over mine, and I peer up at him, lazily trailing my tongue over my lower lip.

"Do you know how badly I want you?"

"Show me."

A sly grin spreads across his face. "Open your mouth for me."

He brushes the tip of his dick over my lips. My tongue slips out, licking the head before sucking him into my mouth, tasting his salty sweetness. He lets out a stream of curse words.

"I swear, the sight of you right now is enough to end this before we even have the chance to get started."

I try not to make it obvious how much it pleases me to hear how much he wants me. Sex with Atlas was always like a race as if we were trying to hurry and see how quickly he could come.

Everything with Corbin is different. More passionate. More intense.

I want to draw it out, enjoy every second of the slow build, knowing we'll find our pleasure together.

He reaches for the button of my jeans, quickly undoing them and slipping them along with my panties off in one fell swoop.

"Lie back for me," he moans, fisting his dick.

I collapse on the bed, my body still positioned on the edge of the mattress, moving my heels up to spread my thighs open for him.

His eyes burn into my pussy before looking up at me. He dips his finger into my heat just barely before brushing the tip over my clit.

"Holy shit." I roll my eyes closed, biting down on my lip.

"Haelynn," he croaks out my name.

I tilt my head to the side, staring down my body at him. He's bent forward, his warm breath heating my wet skin.

"I don't want to lose you."

He moves his fingers over my folds once again, and I'm unable to focus on both at the same time. I trail my fingers over my stomach, then back up underneath the curve of my breast.

"I'd do anything for you and Huxton. I want to take care of you and protect you, for as long as you'll let me."

chapter nineteen

HAELYNN

"Corbin." I reach my hands out toward him, wanting to feel his skin against mine.

I push myself up to my elbows, crawling onto the center of the bed, and he follows me. When he reaches me, he tilts his body over mine. I slowly drag my finger over his chest to his hipbone.

Leaning forward onto his forearms, he brushes my damp hair away from my face and kisses me. He reclines back onto his haunches, lifting my legs and spreading them open.

He dips his finger into my wet heat again, curling his finger up while he rubs his thumb over my clit, sending my back arching. I'm so turned on. My chest heaves from the force of my heavy breaths.

"Please," I moan, holding my arms out toward him.

This time when he leans over me, I don't waste any time. I reach down between us and wrap my fist around him, making it clear exactly what I want. I brush the tip of his dick through my folds, positioning him right where I want him. When he enters me, it's as though all the oxygen has been sucked out of the room.

Neither one of us makes a sound. I slip my arms around his neck, and Corbin presses his body against me. I wrap my legs around his waist, and we both succumb to the moment's intensity.

He reaches for my leg, changing our positions, and rears back, slamming into me. When he stares down at me, his eyes are full of desire. I want to tell him how much he means to me and beg him to never stop.

His finger brushes over my clit as his hips piston in and out. His eyes burn into me while my hand trails over my chest, grabbing my breast and squeezing my nipple between my fingers.

"You're so fucking beautiful, Haelynn."

My vision turns hazy, my release within reach. I want him to finish with me. With one flick of his finger over my clit, his hips thrust into me, and it's enough to send me falling over the edge. My legs tighten around his waist as a rush of sensations races through me before he collapses on top of me.

He moans out my name, mixed with a heavy grunt. His pace picks up before one final thrust, and his body goes slack against mine.

Neither of us moves, but when I finally come back to earth, my fingers begin to draw lazy circles on his back. He goes quiet, and I half expect to hear his breathing even out and the quiet sounds of his snoring signaling he'd fallen asleep.

"I love you."

I wanted to ask him how he could say that and when did it happen? I hate the thought of him regretting those words, especially when he learns the truth, but I also don't want him to go on thinking I didn't feel the same.

"I love you too," I mutter, tears pricking my eyes. I try to blink them away, but it's no use. One slips out, and it's like a dam gives way, sending the rest flowing free down my face.

"Don't cry, baby. It kills me to see you upset," he whispers.

"I'm not sad. I'm happy, but I'm scared."

He pulls back, his brows furrowing in concern. "Why?"

"I just know it's only a matter of time before you realize you deserve so much more than what I can give you."

"No, that won't happen because it'll never be true."

He moves to lie next to me, urging me to follow him. He pulls the blanket over us and wraps his arms around my waist until our tangled limbs are molded perfectly together.

It's long after he's fallen asleep before my body relaxes, and I follow him. When I wake a few hours later, the clock on the nightstand flashes the time. It is three fourteen.

Corbin still hasn't moved an inch. His face is pressed against my back, and his arms are cinched around my waist. I lace my fingers with his and lay there for a while, enjoying the feel of his arms around me.

I know when I get up to leave, I'm going to wish I were back here at this moment with him.

I let out a heavy sigh and unhook his arm, carefully lifting it while trying not to wake him. He shakes his head and mumbles something unintelligible. For a second, I think I'm busted.

He turns, rolling over onto his back, giving me the space to slip out. I stand at the foot of the bed, watching him sleep before I finally have the courage to leave.

I think back to the talk I had with my mom the night before. Her fears of what would happen if anyone found out who my father was and why she had chosen to leave Arbor Creek.

The memory of my conversation with Gage outside the studio, warning me to stay away from him and his friends, flashes through my mind. My father has taken so much from their families already. I don't want to put him in the position to choose between me and the people he loves. It's not fair to him.

When I moved to Arbor Creek, I never expected to meet Corbin. I certainly never thought I'd fall in love with him so quickly.

I force my feet to move out of the bedroom and down the hall toward the front door. An antique desk near the entryway has a pad of paper.

I walk past it and pause, dragging my teeth over my lower lip, contemplating if I want to leave him a note.

The guilt in my stomach brews. He deserves some sort of explanation. I don't think I'd have the strength to tell him face-to-face, and the last thing I want is for him to be left with any questions.

I reach for a pencil from the hutch and press the lead to the paper and write.

Corbin,

I'm sorry to leave the way I did, but I guess I'm once again taking the coward's way out and running. The truth is, I don't know if I have the strength to say this face-to-face. The thought of hurting you makes my heart ache, and I wouldn't be able to handle seeing how different you'd look at me when you found out the truth.

Last night with you was one of the most incredible nights of my life. I will never forget falling asleep in your arms or hearing you tell me you loved me. I've never felt so protected and cared for than when I was with you, and I can't thank you enough for showing me what it means to truly be loved.

There's a lot more about who I am and my past than you know, and I'll never put you in a position to have to choose between me and the people you love.

I'm sorry.

Hae

My eyes scan over the paper, re-reading the words once more. When the pencil touched the paper, it's like the words flowed out of me. I hadn't thought through what I was going to say until I was finished.

I set the pencil back down on the paper and stare at the picture frame on top of the oak desk of Corbin with a man I assume is his older brother, Lee. He's dressed in his army ACU's with Layla flanking the other side, her arm wrapped around Lee's waist and her head against his shoulder.

Tears fill my eyes, and I quickly brush them away, stepping back and hurry out the front door before I can take every word back. I'm careful not to let the screen door slam shut behind me, afraid of waking Corbin as I jog down the stairs toward my car.

During the entire drive home, I picture Corbin opening his eyes that morning to find the bed next to him empty and the sinking feeling I've felt so many times when I've woken up to find Atlas never came home the night before.

I break down at the thought of the familiar ache in the pit of his stomach creeping in, wondering what was wrong. It's just before four in the morning, so I drive back home and attempt to get a few more hours of sleep before I pick up Huxton.

When sleep doesn't come, I pick up my phone from the nightstand next to me and give in to the urge to pull up the photos from our stranger shoot the day we met. I scroll through the album before landing on a picture Madelyn took when Corbin first kissed me.

I'm a mess of emotions as the tears once again blur my vision.

"I'm sorry," I whisper, wishing he could hear me.

Once again, before I allow myself the chance to change my mind, I delete all the pictures from my phone before pulling up our messages and his contact information, and doing the same.

When the pop-up appears on my screen asking to confirm the deletion, my finger hovers over the button before Gage's voice filters through my mind.

"Stay away from him. Stay away from us all."

chapter twenty

CORBIN

I wasn't surprised when I woke up the following morning to find Haelynn gone. I was frustrated and hurt. So instead of jumping out of bed when my alarm went off, I lay there, replaying every second of our night together.

Eventually, I forced myself up and into the shower before I ventured downstairs and found the letter she had left.

A million questions race through my mind.

Instead, I climbed into my truck and took off down the road to spend the day with my parents. My dad and I made plans to go fishing anyway, and I wanted to take advantage of the few warm weekends we had left before it got chilly.

My mom made us breakfast. Layla and Brit brought their kids over to let them run around outside. My aunt Brea and uncle Mason stopped over for a short time before making the trip to Everton to run errands.

It was after noon by the time we made it down to the pond located near the back of their property. Growing up out here, with more land than we knew what to do with, was every boy's dream. My dad kept us busy on the farm, plus we had four-wheelers and dirt bikes, giving us all the space we needed to ride freely.

We spent nearly every day in the summer by the pond they stocked every year. We'd fish, only to release most of them back into the water again.

"How's everything goin'? You seem... quiet. Not yourself," my dad, Callum, asks. He reclines back into his lawn chair, resting his arm on the back of the seat as he turns to look at me.

I cast my line out into the water, balancing my foot up onto the bucket we brought down with our fishing gear. I was still trying to wrap my head around our night together and didn't have the slightest clue where to start.

"You wanna start with this girl you've been seein'?" He must've picked up on my hesitation.

I look over at him with my brow raised. "You've been spyin' on me?"

He scoffs, shaking his head. "Your sister told us all about it after half the world saw those pictures of you kissing her all over that Face Space."

I chuckle. I'm not the least bit surprised to hear Layla was the first to share all the details. There's not enough gossip in her own life, so she keeps up with the rest of the town's juicy secrets and gushes to anyone who cares to listen.

"Is that what's got you in your head?"

"Yeah." I sigh, taking a swig of beer before setting the bottle back on the cooler between us. I hadn't planned on drinking, but when I saw the options of what was packed for us, I figured one or two wouldn't hurt anything.

I could use something to numb the pain.

"Wanna talk about it?"

"Do you remember when you told me about Mom's past, the shit she had gone through before she got on the bus to Arbor Creek?"

He shifts his eyes, staring down at the dock. There was a noticeable change in his demeanor, and he was lost in thought before his eyes flashed back over to me.

"How did you handle it when you tried to be there for her and she pushed you away?"

He chuckles. "You know, it wasn't easy. You're a lot like me. You have this undying need to protect the people you love. When you see someone you care about hurting, you want to jump to action and help them. When they deny your help or push you away, it's hard to wrap your head around why."

I nod. He could read me like a book.

The pain and loss my mom went through is more than anyone should ever have to bear. It wasn't until I was older when my dad sat Liam and me down and told us the full story of what happened before we fully understood.

Even when she was scared and pushed him away, he never gave up on her. He would've given his life to protect her, and when it came down to it, she fought for her life to come back to him.

"It's hard to watch someone you love hurt. At the time, all I could do was stay patient and remind her I wouldn't give up on her. Over time, she slowly began to bring her walls down and let me in."

He had a point. All I could do now was step back and let her come around. I still want to talk to her about her note, knowing that what Gage said at Brodie's is likely weighing on her mind.

"Have you talked to Graham recently?" I ask, adjusting the bill of my cap.

The sun started peeking through the trees, shining into my face. I tilt my head to the side, using the brim to block the sunlight from my eyes.

"Not for a few days. Why, what's up?"

"Gage," I mutter. "We got into a fight earlier this week. I found out some things about Haelynn I hadn't expected to hear, and he didn't handle it well."

He leans forward, staring out into the water before turning to look at me. His eyes narrow, his wheels spinning.

"Haelynn moved to Arbor Creek a few months ago. She grew up in Chicago, but when she got engaged, she and her ex moved here, wanting to be close to family. I guess her mom is from Arbor Creek originally."

This piqued his curiosity, his eyes meeting mine.

"Gage said her father is Marc Krate."

He let out a low whistle, sitting back in his chair. His eyes are wide in surprise.

"I didn't know he even had a daughter..." His voice trails off. "Her mom must be Cindy. She moved away before Marc and Isaac were arrested. She up and took off out of town. No one knew where she went, but it makes sense now. She was protecting her daughter."

"She told me before I ever knew who her father was that her mom moved her away when she got pregnant."

"The police never had any proof Cindy knew anything or was involved in their drug running. When the word got out about what happened, people were angry. It was all anyone talked about around here until they were convicted. I don't blame her for wanting to get away and start over. It was the only way she could protect her daughter from the reality of who her father was."

We sat in silence for a few minutes. The sound of birds chirping and the wind blowing causes leaves to rustle, with the breeze whipping through the alcove.

"How do you feel about it?" he asks.

"Honestly, I think back to our conversation the night she told me about growing up in Chicago. I don't think she was lying or hiding who she was. She told me her dad died in an accident."

"Died in an accident?"

The irony isn't lost on me. "That was her story. I've tried to talk to her, but she won't answer my messages."

He grips the beer bottle in his hand and takes a long pull, staring off into the water. My mind drifts back to the talks we've had about our families.

"You're asking her to trust you, and I think you owe her the same in return. If she did know and she chose not to tell you, you have to wonder if there's a reason. Maybe she wasn't trying to maliciously hurt you. Or maybe she didn't even know."

"I don't think she was trying to hurt me either."

"Give her time, then. You can't pick who your parents are. Knowing Cindy, I think she was doing what she thought was best to shield her from her father and his past. The Krates had an enemy list a mile long."

"She has a son. He's five. You'd love him. He's an awesome kid."

"Really?" He grins. "How do you feel about that? Do you think you're ready to step into that sort of role?"

Every chance I had to spend time with Haelynn and Huxton felt right, like I was right where I was supposed to be.

"You may not be his dad, but your role in his life would be important. It could also factor in to why she has her walls up. You don't want to bring people in and out of your child's life if that person's stay may be temporary."

"You know, if you would've asked me a few months before I met Haelynn if I was ready for a family, I would've laughed in your face. I'd smile and tell you I wasn't ready for kids. Which was true, but I also hadn't met the person I wanted to share my life or start a family with."

His eyes widen, and his brows shot up.

"I don't know what the future has in store, and with how things are right now, I don't want to get too far ahead of myself, but I see a future with Haelynn. I can picture a life with her and Huxton, maybe even a few kids of our own one day. I want that, and more importantly, I want it with her."

He nods, and a smile stretches across his face, his leg bouncing with excitement.

"I'm happy to hear that, son. It makes me proud to see you stepping up for them like you are."

I press my lips together, trying to contain the grin threatening to break across my face. "You and Mom, you'll love him. He's so smart and funny."

"I don't doubt she will. She's been waiting for you and Liam to have kids since, like, yesterday."

My only hope now is the future I can see of us all together will be a reality.

chapter twenty-one

HAELYNN

It's been two weeks now since the incident with Atlas. I've been sitting on pins and needles since. My lawyer filed the paperwork petitioning for full custody of Huxton. He didn't handle it well when I left and took Huxton with me, so I can only imagine how he'll react to this news.

I settle in with a much-needed glass of wine, flipping through episodes of *The Vampire Diaries* on Netflix when my phone vibrates on the couch next to me with a text message.

Madelyn: You up for a girls' night?

Haelynn: Always!

Madelyn: Good, I'm standing at your door. Let me in. LOL!

She's standing on the front step, her hair up in a top knot and a comfy pair of pajamas with her wine bottle clutched under her arm. She has the same thought as I do, and she returns my grin when she sees the glass in my hand.

"Oh, hell yes!" she mutters when she spots Damon and Klaus paused on my TV screen.

"You came over at the right time." I giggle.

"It looks like it," she says, toeing off her shoes and following me into the living room.

I quickly run into the kitchen to grab her a glass before settling back in on the couch, pulling my blanket back over my lap. We've continued to stay busy at the studio. While Gage's words have weighed on me, I haven't let it affect me when it comes to my job.

At the end of the day, I need this job to put food on the table and a roof over our head. I can't just up and walk away from it, even if he wants me to stay away from him and his friends.

I never mentioned the conversation to Madelyn, though, not wanting to put her or Alex in the middle. Lines got blurred when I started seeing Corbin after my first day, but I was trying to remind myself to keep my work and personal life separate.

"I can't tell you how much I need this right now." She sighs, relaxing into her spot.

She pops the cork and pours some into her glass before swirling it around and taking a drink.

"We deserve it." I smile, lifting my glass in cheers before taking a drink myself.

"How have things been going lately?" she asks.

I try to focus my gaze on the TV because, honestly, that was a loaded question. She must notice the thoughts swirling through my mind when she follows it up with more.

"I'm gonna shoot you straight, Hae. You know you don't have to go through all this alone, right? You have Corbin, who wants to be a shoulder for you to lean on, and you have me too."

She's right. I've pushed so many friends away over the years when I was with Atlas. Many of my friends I haven't spoken to in months. I'm used to doing it all alone.

I never want to burden them or my mom with my problems. When I broke down and told her the truth about what was happening at home, I'll never forget the weight I felt lifted off my chest having someone to talk to.

Madelyn has been a damn good friend to me since I moved to Arbor Creek. I had no more than pulled into the driveway when she was showing up for me, helping me unpack and giving me the job at her studio.

"I'm sorry." I stare down at my lap. "You've been amazing to me since we first met. It was never my intention to push you away or make you feel like I didn't appreciate it because I do."

"That's what friends are for." She shrugs. "You don't owe me an apology either. You've had so much on your plate lately. Even when you don't talk about it, I recognize it. I just want you to know you don't have to go through this alone. I'm here for you if you ever want to talk about it."

I nod. "I've been in my head these past few weeks. I guess when I get like that, I tend to shut down. It's just dealing with the divorce and the custody process. Atlas's mood swings stress me out, on top of getting used to life being a single mom. Then there's Corbin…" I trail off.

"I also found out some news recently about my father. News I wasn't expecting to hear that has shaken me up. It puts me in a difficult place with you, Corbin, and your friends."

"Alex told me."

My eyes dart up to meet hers, surprised.

"I should backtrack and say Alex has been coming home grumbling a lot lately over Gage. He's been moody, and it's made their working relationship… well, rough. Alex is so easy to get along with, though. He goes with the flow, so it's virtually impossible to get him worked up. He didn't give me many details, but he mentioned Gage told him your father was connected to the accident that killed his uncle."

I take another drink of my wine. I'm going to need more if we are going to go all in on this conversation. Madelyn laughs when I gulp it down, reaching across the coffee table to grab the bottle and holding it out to me to refill my glass.

"Until a few weeks ago, I thought I lost my father in an accident. I didn't have any idea he was connected to his uncle, or his relationship to Gage and Corbin. Hell, I didn't know anything about all of this." I gesture with my hands, shaking my head.

"I mean, how would you? C'mon, that happened so long ago. Not to mention, it's not like you came to town set on causing any hurt from it. The accident is in no way your fault."

The anxiety I've been feeling over this conversation eases up. I still haven't talked to Corbin about it. I don't know when I ever will, but it helps to know Madelyn sees my perspective.

"It just adds another layer on top of everything else going on. The last thing I want is for my intentions to be misunderstood. I have no idea where Gage ever got the impression I came here for the wrong reasons, but the fact he insinuated I did bothers me."

"Is this why you've been pushing Corbin away?"

"Part of it." My heart squeezes in my chest. "It felt like everything was happening so fast. One second, I find out about the accident and who my father truly is, the past my mother has been working to cover up my entire life. Then the next, I'm dealing with Atlas at my door, drunk and grabbing me while my son is down the hall. I just needed to take a step back and remember my focus needs to stay on Huxton. He's what is important right now."

She nods. "You're right. He should come first above all you're doing, but Haelynn, so should you. I know I don't have all the details of what happened when you were with Atlas or what brought you here specifically, but I do know you. I think you've spent so much time covering up and hiding from how you feel, putting Huxton at the forefront of your mind, you've forgotten to make sure you're happy too.

"I don't blame you at all for wanting to take a step back. All I'm saying is it shouldn't have to be one or the other. Don't you think you deserve to be happy too?"

Tears prick my eyes. She's right. It's been so long since I've focused on myself that I've almost forgotten what that's like. She reaches her hand out toward me, folding it on top of mine, and squeezes it.

"Does Corbin make you happy?"

The tear streams down my face, and my lip trembles, responding with a subtle nod. "It scares me."

She leans over to set her glass on the table before sliding across the couch toward me, wrapping me in a warm hug.

"He's one of the good ones, Hae. I promise, they don't get any better than Corbin."

"Why does he have to be so damn perfect?" I retort, and Madelyn pulls back, laughing.

"I can picture him shooting you a wink and saying something sweet with the word darlin' hanging on the end."

"He sure knows how to sweet-talk a woman's pants right off." I giggle.

This time, Madelyn tosses her head back, and we both laugh before she smacks her hand over her mouth. "I need to be quiet before I wake up Huxie."

I grin. That kid sleeps like a rock, though, so I'm sure he'll be okay.

"Seriously, though, I want you to know I'm here for you. If you need someone to talk to about how you're feeling or someone to help with Huxton, I'm here. Or even when you don't want to talk but want the company. I'm always down for wine and movies. You're not alone, Hae. Not anymore."

"Thank you." I flash her a small smile.

Luck was on my side the day I met Madelyn.

We both get sucked into watching TV again. The conversation turns easy, chatting about our favorite celebrity crushes and fictional characters before shifting to talk about the upcoming Halloween party she was throwing in a few weeks.

Conversations with Madelyn always feel easy. She has a way of reading you and knows precisely what to say to make you feel better. It was something I noticed about her the very first day we met.

The episode ends, and I reach for the remote to start the next one when she breaks through the silence to ask, "So have you heard from Corbin lately?"

The way she words it makes it seem like she already knows the answer, but I pretend I didn't hear it and shake my head.

She chuckles. "All right, I'll cut the bull. I already knew. He's called and texted me a few times, wanting to see how you were doing. I think you should sit down with him and tell him what you told me. If anything, he deserves to hear the truth. At least give him a chance to tell you how he feels. If you still feel like you're not ready right now, you can move forward on good terms. Ya know?"

"You're right." I press my lips together. "I've been avoiding the conversation out of fear, but he deserves to know the truth."

"I think the conversation will go better than you think," she reassures.

My phone lights up, vibrating on the coffee table, and my heart leaps at the thought of it being Corbin. I quickly swipe it, checking to see who it's from.

"Madelyn," I blurt out.

"What?"

"He just texted me."

I lift my glass of wine, taking a heavy gulp before clutching it against my chest. It's as though I was trying to hold myself together, afraid at any moment I'll fall apart.

"What'd he say?"

"He said he got my letter and has been thinking about what I said. He asked if we could still talk face-to-face."

"He's not going to let you go so easily. He's fighting for his girl." She grins. "You should ask him if he wants to come over to talk."

"Right now?" I stare down at my phone, checking the time. It's a quarter to ten. The thought of seeing Corbin has my heart beating in overdrive.

She moves to stand and tells me she's going to take off. She gives me a hug and reassures me once again it will all work out how it's supposed to before I walk her to the door.

I'm standing in the entryway, where we were the day of the bonfire, re-reading our conversation before I work up the nerve to press send on my message.

Me: Want to come over now?

Corbin: On my way.

Me: See you soon.

I quickly pick up my blankets and carry the glasses into the kitchen, depositing them into the sink before I race into my bedroom to freshen up. It will only take him a few minutes to get here.

A part of me hopes Madelyn is right. Even when I open up and tell him the truth, he still won't let me go.

And, for once in my life, he'll make me feel like I'm worth fighting for.

CORBIN

The sky is dark, with only the ominous glow of the street-lamp on the corner and the light outside of Haelynn's front door lighting the street. I pull up in front of Haelynn's house and put my truck in park, hearing the rustling of leaves crunch beneath my boots when I step out.

I shoot off a text to let her know I'm here, not wanting to wake Huxton if I were to knock. A few seconds later, the door cracks open, and her face and dark brown hair peek outside.

The sight of her again sends my heart hammering in overdrive. It's so good to see her, but I can't ignore the way my stomach churns and my chest tightens, wondering how our conversation will go.

When I reach the steps, she holds the door open for me. When I step into the entryway, I pause in front of her, searching her face for any sign of how she's doing and where this conversation may go.

"How are you?" I whisper, trying to be quiet.

"I'm okay." She smiles hesitantly. I kick off my shoes and shed my coat, hanging it on the rack near the door.

She crosses her arms in front of her and tangles her fingers together, fidgeting, before she folds her arms over her chest. I'm unable to resist the urge to hold her, so I reach out and pull her into my arms. I practically sigh in relief when she comes to me easily, circling her arms around my waist.

"I've missed this," I murmur, tracing my nose along the side of her face, inhaling her scent. The familiar smell eases the tension coiled inside me.

The fact I'm even here with her in my arms is a step in the right direction.

"I've missed you." She exhales. The words come out fast, almost as if she hadn't expected to say them but couldn't hold them in any longer.

"It's hard going into the studio and remembering when we first met. I try to focus on working, but I'm reminded of you every time another notification appears on our pictures. People all over the world are still commenting on them. If you think for a second this has been easy for me, or this is what I've wanted, you're wrong."

I lean my head back, brushing my fingers through her hair, and press a kiss against her lips to stop her. She sucks in a deep breath, and her fingers grip the front of my shirt, holding on and not letting go.

She opens her mouth to me, and our tongues tangle together. I swear, at this moment, I don't care about anything else but her.

I don't care about the past, what's happened, or any of the reasons this may not work out between us. I don't care who would be upset or disappointed by me wanting her or the hurt it could cause.

None of it matters because when I'm near her, when I feel her skin beneath my hands and her body molds against mine, I feel whole in ways I never knew were missing.

When we break apart, I tilt my forehead against hers and suck in a deep breath, trying to calm my racing heart.

She slides her fingers into mine, and I follow her into the living room. She's made some changes since the last time I was here. Art hangs on the wall above the couch with new photos of her and Huxton on the end table.

What doesn't escape my notice is the picture frame next to it from our photo shoot with my arms wrapped around her.

The sight of the photo causes my breath to get caught in my chest. My eyes bounce over to hers, and she holds her fingers in front of her mouth, staring at the picture before looking back up at me.

"C'mere," I murmur, guiding her with me onto the couch, sliding her legs over mine. She circles her arms around me, resting her head against my shoulder.

The room was dim, with only the lamp on the end table and a candle flickering on the coffee table.

"I'm sorry for leaving like I did the next morning."

"Why did you?"

"It's just..." She trails off, pausing to rub her fingers over her eyes. "I guess I was scared. I'm scared of what I need to tell you, scared of wanting this too much, of opening my son up to the idea of you only for it to be taken away."

I reach for her hand, tangling our fingers together, and she continues.

"Haelynn, you should know I already know who your father is. I knew the night you came over and stayed with me. Don't you think if I knew and it was a deal breaker, I wouldn't have let it go that far?"

She slips her hand out of mine and clenches it into a fist, collapsing back against the couch.

"You have to understand, my marriage with Atlas was like living every day waiting for the other shoe to drop, for his switch to flip. When Gage came to see me at the studio, I just, I don't know. I guess I just lost it."

Gage went to see her?

"When did he come see you?"

"The day Atlas attacked you, right as I was leaving work. I need you to know I didn't know a lot about my father, or what he did to Gage's uncle. I swear, I didn't. I would never keep that from you."

A pained look crosses her face, and a tear slips from her eye, trailing down her cheek.

"I know you didn't," I assure her, tilting her head back to look me in the eye. "This happened a long time ago, long before either of us was born. Even if you did know, what happened to his uncle is not your fault."

Her body trembles with the emotions erupting out of her, and tears pour down her face.

"I've never known who my father truly was. Until last week, when I finally spoke to my mom, the story I had been told was that he'd been the one who died in the accident. Not Gage's uncle."

I wrap my arms around her, attempting to calm her and remind her I'm here. To sit here with her and see how hard the news has rocked her, it makes sense why she may have clung to her relationship with Atlas for so long. She didn't want Huxton to miss out on the opportunity to have his dad in his life and for them to be a family.

"I always questioned the story my mom told me. Why didn't she give me his last name? Why wasn't he mentioned on my birth certificate?"

"She didn't want you to be burdened with the truth."

She nods. "I remember her taking me to see him when I was younger. She told me he was a friend of hers who went away for doing bad things. Memories from that day have started to come back to me. He was upset with her for bringing me with her. I was shocked by the way he spoke to her when she told him to take a good look at me because he'd never see me again. She didn't think I heard her, but I did."

"He looked me straight in the eyes. He had dark circles underneath them, void of any emotion. He didn't say a word to me. He stood and pounded on the door, and without a second glance, they took him away."

I didn't want to tell her what I knew, not wanting to pain her with the truth.

Graham, Gage's father, didn't shy away from telling him the reason he opened Compass Security. The Krates were known for their involvement in running drugs through

Iowa. His uncle worked as a police officer in Arbor Creek as well and got information about a job.

Rumors were running around he was involved in trafficking women. When he started poking around and asking questions, it ticked the Krates off. They wanted him off their trail, but he didn't back down when they threatened him. If anything, it only got worse.

Graham was behind putting the Krates in prison, something that no doubt made a mark on him.

"Sometimes people don't turn out to be who we thought they were." I pause, looking over at her. "Sometimes things don't work out how we hope they will either, and that's okay too."

She nods, her body deflating against the couch.

"I meant what I've said from the beginning. I'm not going anywhere. I'm not only here through the fun stage or when it's easy. I'd never walk away from you either, especially when you need me the most."

She purses her lips, blinking through the tears forming in her eyes.

"I know you're scared, and I understand why, but you don't need to be. Not with me."

She adjusts her position, moving her leg over to straddle my lap. I guide her body closer to me, slipping my arms around her waist and ducking my head into the curve of her neck. She wraps her arms around mine, holding me against her while her body trembles with the emotions flowing out of her.

The room falls silent, and all I'm able to think about is how badly I've missed her and how much I've needed this when two knocks pound against the front door.

She pulls back, quickly climbing to her feet. She seems frantic, concerned about who it could be.

"Do you want me to answer it?" I ask, sensing her unease.

She walks toward the window, peering through the curtains before turning on her heel, her eyes wide.

"It's Atlas," she mouths.

"It's okay," I assure her, just as two more knocks bang against the door. This time much louder.

She grits her teeth, muttering under her breath about how he's going to wake up Huxton intermixed with a stream of swear words.

She glances back at me when she hits the lock on the door. I stand behind the wall, separating the living room from the entryway, motioning for her not to worry because I'll be right here.

We both know if he had any inkling I was here, it would only cause more of a scene.

I'm able to see the door if I were to take a quick sidestep. Unless he's looking for me, he likely wouldn't see me.

She nods, releasing a deep breath before turning the door handle and opening the door.

"What are you doing here?" she whisper-shouts at him, her voice firm.

I'm unable to make out what he says when she quickly follows it up with, "Have you been drinking again?"

I peer around the corner to find Atlas bent over at the waist, his hands on his knees, shaking his head. When he finally stands up and reaches for the door, he stumbles back for a second before righting himself.

She's right. It looks like he's drunk, and judging by the look on his face, he's upset. His eyes are red and swollen, puffy as though he's been crying.

He pulls the screen door open and steps toward Haelynn, but she puts her hand up between them to stop him from coming any farther.

"You can't just show up here whenever you want, unannounced. Huxton is asleep, and I don't want to talk to you right now."

"Haelynn," Atlas begs. "I got the petition for custody today. Please, just talk to me. I'm sorry."

His words are broken up, his voice quivering with emotion. He is clearly torn up and not in a good way.

"Atlas, no. It's not a good time."

"Why?" he commands, his voice growing loud. "Why are you doing this to us?"

"Atlas, I'm not kidding. You can sit down on the steps and call an Uber or someone to come give you a ride, but you need to go. I'm not doing this with you. What's done is done. What I want from you now is to take care of you first so you can focus on being a better person and father to your son."

He turns, appearing to accept her answer, but something halts his movement.

When he turns back around, the look on his face has changed from one of sadness into something darker. Haelynn must sense the shift in his demeanor. She reaches for the door handle to pull it closed behind her as Atlas stops her.

"Is it because he's here with you? Is that why you won't talk to me?"

"Atlas, I'm not kidding. You need to go."

Her voice grows louder and more urgent, attempting to yank the door closed.

"No, tell me. He's here with you, isn't he? In the house with *my* son? How could you do this to me? How can you move on and let some man into our son's life and try to replace me? I'm his father."

"Who I spend my time with is none of your business, Atlas. Huxton knows you're his father. He needs you to be his father. Now, please, I'm only going to say this to you once more. You need to go, or I'm going to call the police."

"I can't lose you," he pleads, reaching out to grab her. She shoves him back.

I've seen enough.

"You need to go. Now!" I command, stepping behind Hae-lynn. Her body trembles, stepping behind me. "She told you to leave. You need to listen to what she says and go."

He runs his fingers through his hair, jerking his head away. His jaw set, and his body taut.

I don't notice right away until he's pulling his hand out of his pocket. Before I have the chance to stop him, he's whipping his pocketknife open, and it's too late.

I only have enough time to push Haelynn out of the way, using my body to shield her from him when he lunges toward me.

He's drunk and stumbling, so I'm able to dodge his swing.

"Atlas, no! Please! Don't do this," she begs.

His eyes burn into me, down to where my arm stretches out to push her away, protecting her from him. They are wide and maniacal, jolting back to meet mine.

He bares his teeth, and the vein in his forehead protrudes, growing red.

"Calm down, man. You don't want to do this." I attempt to persuade him. "I know you're upset, but this isn't how you want to handle things. You don't want to hurt anyone, right? Let's take a deep breath and calm down."

Through the shouting and commotion, I notice a light across the street flick on, and Alex steps out onto his front porch. He's dressed in a T-shirt and a pair of shorts.

He holds his hand up to me, signaling to keep him calm as he darts back into the house.

When my eyes dart back to Atlas, a slow grin stretches across his face.

"That's where you're wrong." He chuckles, lunging toward me once more. This time, Haelynn steps away. The strong stench of blood hits me as I collapse against the wall.

It's not until he pulls the blade out and I hear Haelynn's cries wailing behind me, sending me crumpling to the floor, that I comprehend what's happening.

"You took from me what is mine, and I'd love nothing more than to watch you suffer."

chapter twenty-two

CORBIN

The sight of blood pouring from Corbin, drenching his shirt, sends me collapsing to my knees. I recall the sound of Atlas's laughter before he took off, running toward his car.

After that, everything was a blur. All I can remember is sitting with Corbin's head in my lap, begging him to hold on and not to leave me.

"I'm not going anywhere," I promise him when they load him into the ambulance. "I'll meet you at the hospital."

Madelyn urges me into the back with him, reassuring me not to worry. She took my phone and quickly entered my mom's number into hers.

"I'll stay here with Huxton until I get ahold of your mom. Don't worry, I won't let anything happen to him."

Corbin was rushed into the emergency room to assess his injuries when we got to the hospital. I sat in the hallway, waiting. Every minute that passed felt like it ticked by at an agonizingly slow pace.

I lean against the cool brick wall and slide to the floor, wrapping my arms around my legs and burying my head in my lap. My body trembles with the emotions racing through me, unable to contain it any longer.

"There she is." I hear Alex's voice coming from the end of the hall, standing next to an older man and woman.

The woman has light blond hair and tan skin. The man next to him, though, was like staring into the future. From the way he stood to his body structure to the dark hair intermixed with his five o'clock shadow, there was no doubt he was Corbin's father.

"Oh, sweetheart," the woman cries, racing toward me. She bends down on the floor in front of me, wrapping her arms around me in a warm hug.

I know without introduction that she's Corbin's mom. My chin trembles, and my chest tightens with fear of what could happen to her son.

"It's going to be okay," she reassures me, rubbing her hand over my back. "We have to believe he will be okay."

She pulls back, flashing me a warm smile before pushing herself to her feet and holding her hand out to help me up.

"I'm Corbin's mom. You can call me Ellie, and this is his dad, Callum." She squeezes my hand reassuringly before taking a step back.

"Corbin has told us so much about you, Haelynn, and that son of yours. I feel like we know you already." Her warm voice is so comforting.

"He's going to be all right," Callum's gruff voice adds. "He's too stubborn not to be."

A smile breaks across Ellie's face, nodding in agreement. "Ain't that the truth."

She drapes her arms around Callum's waist, and he runs his hand over her back. He leans into her ear, whispering something to her. I couldn't help but picture Corbin and me together when I see the two of them. The only difference is the color of my hair.

Corbin has told me so much about his mom, her past, and what led her to Arbor Creek, where she met his dad.

"Their story has always kept me believing no matter what obstacles are put in your way, no matter what life has thrown you, there's always a light at the end of a dark tunnel."

"What do we know yet? Or are we still waiting?" Callum asks.

"They're doing an ECG right now. They are worried about the amount of blood he lost. He may need a transfusion," Alex says as the door at the end of the hall opens, and Madelyn comes rushing through.

She turns back and mutters to someone we're down this way. A moment later, I spot Gage turn the corner behind her. My eyes flash to Alex and release a deep breath. He winks before flashing me a reassuring smile as if saying it's okay.

The closer Madelyn gets to us, the more I see her blood-shot eyes from the tears she's shed.

"Any word on Grey and if they found him yet?" Alex asks Gage, referring to Atlas by our last name. I drag my teeth over my lower lip, a ball of guilt lodged in my throat.

I tip my head down, staring at the tile floor. The mention of Atlas and what he did has my stomach twisting in knots all over again.

"I'm so sorry," I choke out. "I would never want anything to happen to Corbin."

"Haelynn, this isn't your fault. Please don't beat yourself up over this." Ellie attempts to reassure me.

"She's right. Sometimes people do bad things we'll never understand," Callum interjects. His voice is hard, commanding. "Corbin wouldn't want you to blame yourself for this, either. This isn't your fault, and *no one* here thinks so."

He emphasizes the words "no one." The silence that falls over the group is deafening. I almost wonder if everyone else can hear my heart race, the sound flooding my ears.

The urge to glance over at Gage eats away at me, knowing what Callum just said was untrue. Gage hated my father for his part in killing his uncle, and I don't doubt for a second he blames me for what happened to Corbin.

"Isn't that right, Gage?" Callum says, cutting to the chase.

My head jerks up, staring at him. A solemn look falls over his face, avoiding my gaze. It takes a second before he nods his head, peering over to look at me.

"Yes, sir," Gage agrees. "This isn't your fault, Haelynn."

Madelyn reaches out, and I sag into her, slipping my arm around her waist in a hug.

"It's okay," she soothes me. She whispers in my ear that she'll always be here for me and stay with me for as long as I need her.

When we finally break apart, she runs her thumbs beneath my eyes, wiping away the mascara streaking down my face.

"Huxton's okay. He woke up shortly after you left. He needed to use the bathroom, not from the commotion or anything. When I heard his bedroom door open, I went to check on him and told him you had to leave for a bit. I told him your mom would be with him when he woke up, and you'd be home later."

"Thank you." I sigh. "I'm glad he didn't hear anything."

"Alex took care of talking with the police. They have someone staying outside in case he tries to come back. For now, they're focusing on finding Atlas."

"I just can't believe this," I whisper.

Time continues to drag on the longer we sit in the waiting area. Every time the door opens, my eyes dart over in hopes it's someone coming to give us an update.

"Haelynn, I know this may not be the best time, but do you want to go for a walk with me? We can get a cup of coffee while we wait," Gage asks.

He slips his hands in his pockets. My eyes dart over to Madelyn and Alex before looking at Gage.

"We'll make it quick," he assures me. "I know you don't want to be gone too long."

Madelyn promises to text me if the doctor gives any updates. I nod, walking with Gage down the hallway, a silence falling over the two of us.

"It's long past the time I admit I owe you an apology."

I peer over at Gage, not expecting an apology from him. I don't say anything, not wanting to interrupt him, so I let him continue.

"I'm sorry. I will admit I misjudged your intentions when you first came to town and started spending time with Corbin. The guys have given me a lot of grief lately, asking questions and wanting to know what's changed in me. There's a lot I can't discuss on a case we worked a few months back, but it, ahh…" His voice trails off as if trying to find the right words.

He lifts his thumb and rubs it over his lower lip, lost in thought.

"This last job, though, I went undercover for a bit to try to get some intel. I met someone and, well, I guess you can say things didn't end well for us. I can't be mad at her because neither of us was honest with who we were, but it fucked with me. I barely made it out of there alive."

Gage's voice cracks as he shares bits and details of his story about meeting and falling in love, only to learn it was a lie. I think back to the day of the bonfire and how different his tone was toward me and how Corbin reassured me he hasn't been himself.

"I meant what I said back there, though. What happened to Corbin and what happened to my uncle are not your fault. Corbin is one of the best men I know. He's loyal and would fight for the people he loves. There's no doubt in my mind he'd put himself before you to protect you any day. Not only because it's the man he is, but because he loves you."

My phone vibrates, and I reach out, gripping Gage's arm to stop him. Madelyn's name flashes on my screen with an unread message.

Madelyn: He's okay. Doctor came out to talk to us and assured us he'll be fine. He's awake and waiting for you.

"He's awake."

I don't even bother to wait for Gage or check if he's following me before I take off down the hall back where we came from.

All I care about is getting back to where I belong, back to Corbin, and telling him I love him, and I always will.

chapter twenty-four

CORBIN

All my life I've had one foot on the gas. I like to get out of the house and stay busy. When I was finally released from the hospital under strict orders to take it easy, I gave the doc one look and said, "Yeah, all right."

He peered over at Haelynn and sternly replied, "I mean it. Keep an eye on him."

It turns out the knife narrowly missed my spleen, which could've done much more damage if it had been punctured. They ended up giving me a blood transfusion because of how much I'd lost and kept me for a couple of days to keep an eye on my recovery. I'm relieved it wasn't any worse than it could've been.

When I finally busted out, Haelynn insisted I come home with her. Madelyn didn't even bat an eye when she asked if she could work from home for a bit until I was back on my feet.

I'm not one to be coddled. I've taken care of myself this long, but dammit if I didn't love having Haelynn as my nurse.

She insisted on me staying in her bed while she slept on the couch. I was damn near ready to carry her to the room with me when she put her foot down and demanded I knock it off. I agreed to let it go for the night, but when she snuck into bed with me after Huxton was asleep, I realized she was only saying it for his sake.

Going to sleep next to her every night and waking up to her beautiful smile is becoming my favorite part of the day.

We still haven't talked about what the future has in store for the two of us. For now, we're focusing on being there for each other, and we'll figure it out in time.

My sergeant called to check in on me and assured me they had captured Atlas. He was currently sitting in jail, waiting to be arraigned on his charges. It was a long road ahead, but all I cared about was knowing he was behind bars and couldn't show up here. More importantly, I knew he wouldn't be able to hurt Haelynn or Huxton next.

Haelynn left a few minutes ago to take Huxton to school. I'm standing in the kitchen, fixing a bowl of cereal, when I hear two knocks on the front door.

It's hard for me to take a deep breath, so moving around the house isn't easy. I amble toward the door. Peering through the peephole, I spot Gage standing on the other side. He's wearing a dark-gray beanie with his hands in his pockets.

I flip the lock and hold the door open to him, letting him inside.

"Hey, man!"

"Sorry to bother you. I was hoping you and Haelynn may be around. How are ya feelin'?"

"I'm hangin' in there." I glance over my shoulder.

Gage toes off his shoes by the door and follows me into the kitchen.

"How's Haelynn handling everything?"

"Honestly, she seems to be doing okay. She keeps worrying over me and Huxton. She had a sit-down conversation with him to explain how I got hurt and how his dad will be going away for a while."

Gage grits his teeth, forcing a smile. "I don't envy her there."

I finish pouring my bowl of cereal, close the box, and put it away before grabbing milk from the fridge.

"Man, neither do I. We've been keeping an eye on him. She's been talking about getting him in to see a counselor, someone to check in to make sure he's doing okay. Huxton's a good kid, though. He's resilient and seems to be handling things as good as you could hope, given the situation."

"I can't even imagine." Gage's voice drops, staring past me for a moment. He shakes his head, climbing up to take a seat on the barstool across from me.

"He asked if he'd ever see his dad again, which is a hard question to answer. I stepped out of the room and gave her space, but I could hear her struggling to tell him he would likely be in jail for a long time."

The front door opening interrupts our conversation, followed by the sound of Haelynn singing, "Hello, it's me," down the hall. I'm shoving a spoonful of cinnamon squares into my mouth when she sees Gage sitting across from me.

"Gage, hi. I didn't know you were here."

Her face turns red at her rendition of Adele. Haelynn mentioned she had talked to Gage briefly in the hospital before it got cut short.

"I'm sorry." Gage chuckles. "I'm ridin' with Alex to Everton for a job, so I walked over here from the office. I won't be too long. I know you have to get to work too."

"Oh, it's okay. Is everything all right?" Haelynn asks, circling the island to stand next to me. She reaches her hand out, rubbing my back soothingly while focusing her attention on Gage.

"I just, before everything happened, I said some things to both of you that were out of line. We all know the connections our families have to each other, but what happened had nothing to do with anyone in this room. I'm sorry for what I said and did, but more importantly, I'm sorry for how it put a strain on your relationship."

I set the bowl down on the counter and reach my hand down to grab Haelynn's, squeezing it in mine.

"You don't owe me an apology personally. I know you came from a good place. You thought you were lookin' out for me. Next time, come and talk to me, though, and trust me enough to make the right decision."

I step past Haelynn and circle to the other side of the island, pulling Gage into a hug. When I pull back, I see remorse etching his features just before I turn to Haelynn.

"Same here," Haelynn says. "I understand your loyalty to your friends and family. I commend you for it, honestly. You were protecting the people you love, but I can assure you,

you don't need to protect Corbin from me. I never want to hurt him or any of you for that matter."

"I know, and if I'm being honest, I knew that even back then too."

Haelynn steps around me, wrapping her arm around Gage in a friendly hug.

"All right." I clear my throat, jokingly pulling her back into my arms by the waist. "That's enough hugging for today. Unless you want to give me one, baby."

I raise my brows suggestively, dragging my teeth over my lower lip. Haelynn playfully swats me on the arm, shaking her head.

"I have to set up for my work shift, so I have to get going. I'll leave you two alone, in case you want to hug it out some more."

"Listen here, woman," I holler from behind her. Her fit of giggles filters down the hallway.

Gage hangs out for a bit longer, talking about the Hawk-eye football game this weekend against Ohio State. We make plans for him to stop by and grill some burgers. He ends up ducking out a few minutes later, needing to head to Compass himself.

I sneak in and out of Haelynn's office throughout the day. The first few times, she shoos me away, using the doctor's orders excuse. When she steps out on her lunch break, though, all bets were off.

I had it all planned out with her lunch cooking away in the oven. She had leftovers from the night before when we ordered takeout from Brodie's while I ate Haelynn for lunch.

"What am I going to do with you?"

I lift my finger to my mouth, sucking on it before licking my lips. Heat flames her face. She presses her palms against her warm skin, attempting to cover her embarrassment.

"I can think of a few things…" I grin. "We'll need more time, though."

After a few weeks of staying with Haelynn, we agreed it was best for me to go back and stay at my place, as hard as it was for me to do. The time with her had brought us closer together, along with my relationship with Huxton.

We agreed moving so quickly, especially under the circumstances, had the potential of ruining what we had. I still made it a point to stop by a few nights a week to have dinner with her and Huxton. On the nights when I don't, I stop by after she puts him to bed to spend time with her alone.

I stick to my promise, assuring her I wasn't going anywhere, and we'd go at whatever pace she needed from here.

Tonight, we decided to order pizza from a small place just outside of Arbor Creek. I picked it up after work while she grabbed Huxton on her way home, and we'd meet back at her place.

It is just after five when I pull into the driveway, parking behind Haelynn. Before I had a chance to knock on the door, Huxton smacks his hands against the door and presses his small nose against the glass.

"What are you doing, kid?"

"Nothin'." He shrugs, stepping back to let me through. He zooms past me, his arms out like an airplane racing toward the kitchen.

Haelynn stood at the sink, washing off a plate before setting it in the dish drainer beside her. Her eyes light up when she sees me. Seeing her after being away all day makes me eager to pull her into my arms.

I set the pizza box on the island and cross the room, stepping up behind her and gripping her hips in my hands.

"Corbin," she chastises me, peering over to see Huxton sitting at the island with his Lego blocks scattered over the granite countertop in front of him.

"He's not even paying attention," I whisper, pulling her into a hug. She slips her arms around me, and I sneak a kiss against the column of her neck.

She sucks in a sharp breath, her body trembling against me. I don't regret it, but damn if it's not making it hard to step back, knowing little eyes and ears were a few feet away.

"Corbin?" Huxton says, my name coming out as more of a question.

"What's up, buddy?" I ask, opening the cabinet next to Haelynn to grab a few paper plates and tossing them by the pizza box.

"Are you and my mom boyfriend and girlfriend?"

I glance at Haelynn out of the corner of my eye. It takes mental effort to keep myself composed. The serious look on his face makes me want to chuckle.

"If we were, how would you feel about that?"

He rests his chin on his small fist, appearing to consider it for a moment before a smile stretches across his face.

"I think it'd be pretty cool."

"Yeah?"

He nods. "Yeah. Does that mean you're gonna fall in love and get married?"

Haelynn crosses her arms and presses her fingers against her mouth, attempting to smother her smile.

"I mean, I hope so."

"Me too." He nods, bouncing in his seat. "She's happier when you're here. She smiles a lot and stuff."

Tears well up in Haelynn's eyes. She does her best to blink through them, trying to keep it together.

"She makes me happier than I've ever been in my whole life. There's nowhere in the world I'd rather be than here with you two. I'll want to be here for you both, to take care of you and keep you safe."

Huxton smiles, looking over at his mom. He jumps down from his chair and runs over to wrap his arms around her waist.

"Don't cry, Mommy," Huxton whispers. "It's gonna be all right now."

Any hope of Haelynn keeping it together went out the window with that one simple sentence. She drops to her knees and wraps her arms around him in a hug.

I'd put my life on the line every day to protect them.

I'd sacrifice it all to keep them safe.

"Thank you for watching Huxton for us." I smile when Madelyn pulls me in for a hug. "I don't know what I'd do without you these last few months."

It's the truth. We've continued to grow closer over the past few weeks since the night of our talk. I can't imagine how differently my life would be right now had I not moved across the street from her.

"Of course! I love that little turd."

She pulls back and glances over at Huxton. She recently shared that she and Alex are trying to have their little one, so she'd gladly take him for us whenever Corbin and I want a date night.

When Corbin got wind of that, he was ready to cash in on the offer. We've been seeing each other for three months and still haven't gone on a date with just the two of us.

When we heard the temperatures were supposed to be in the low seventies, which is warm for Iowa, Corbin insisted on us having a night just the two of us. He wouldn't share much, but he was excited about his plans.

"I left a spare key to our place in Huxton's bag."

She smiles and waves me off, telling me to have fun before she joins Huxton. He has his Hot Wheels scattered across the living room floor. They are both too enthralled to pay me any mind as I slip out the door.

Corbin waits at the end of my driveway.

"You ready?" he asks, raising his brow.

"We have the night to ourselves. I'm all yours now."

"Mm," he moans, slipping his arms around my waist and pressing his lips to mine. I almost forget we're outside when he pulls back.

"We should get going before Mary Jean comes outside and threatens to call the cops on us."

I toss my head back, laughing. "We're not breaking any laws, officer. I swear."

"If we keep this up, though, we will be. I'm not trying to get in trouble, nor do I want to lose my job."

I grin, shaking my head. He opens the door to his pickup and watches as I climb in.

"Don't forget to buckle up."

"Yes, sir." My voice drops low. His face falls, and he grumbles under his breath something about spanking my ass before he slams the door and jogs around the front to join me.

I peer out the window behind the bench seat, spotting an air mattress in the truck bed. It's hard to see with the sun setting and darkness starting to fall over the night sky.

"Where are we going, and why do you have a bed in the back?"

"It's a surprise." He grins, backing out of the driveway.

It's a short trip, and I'm even more confused when we pull onto the road leading toward Corbin's house before turning into his drive.

"You're taking me to your house for our date?"

"Patience, woman."

He drives slowly past his shop, the crunching of the gravel under the tires the only sound between us. When he veers off into the grass along the side of the barn, I glance over at him, silently wondering what the heck he has up his sleeve.

I lean forward to peer out the windshield. A white sheet was draped along the side of the worn and rustic building. He turns, backing in so the tailgate faces the barn.

"Give me a minute to get everything set up," Corbin says, a broad smile stretching across his face.

I lean back, resting against the headrest, and close my eyes. It's been a long road to where I am now, but I thank my lucky stars every day Corbin was brought into my life.

The seconds tick by, but I keep my eyes faced forward, not wanting to ruin the surprise. A few minutes later, the door handle pops, and Corbin stands beside me. He leans into the cab, tilting my head toward him, and presses his soft lips against mine.

This time he doesn't pull back. Our tongues tangle together in a duel, causing my chest to heave with every strangled breath. He reaches his hand across my lap and unbuckles the seat belt before stepping back, holding his hand out to help me out.

When I turn to face the truck, music plays, illuminating a picture against the makeshift screen.

"We're going to watch a movie?" My eyes light up.

When Corbin was recovering, Huxton loved making forts in the living room. Corbin would crawl in to watch movies with him. It was something they did to bond together. The forts continued to grow until they nearly took over the entire room.

Atlas hardly ever made time for Huxton, so when Corbin came into his life and gave him nothing but his time, I could see how much it meant to Huxton. He was building a bond with him that meant the world to both of us.

I press my hand to my chest, amazed at the thought he put into making the night special. He reaches for my other hand, guiding me to climb over the tailgate and onto the bed. Pillows and blankets cover the back with small lights draped along the side, twinkling in the darkness, giving it a cozy and romantic feeling.

Corbin crawls behind me, reclining against the pillows before pulling me into his arms. The warmth from our body heat mixed with the cool breeze sends goose bumps skating across my skin. Corbin thought it all through and pulled a blanket over us as we cuddled in.

His arms wrap around me, his fingers tracing a path over my arms. The more his hands begin to roam, the more distracted I've become.

I tilt my head back against his shoulder, staring over at him to find him looking back at me. He grips my chin in his fingers, kissing me once more. It starts off slow and sensual before his mouth opens to trace his tongue along my lower lip. When I open my mouth to him, he brushes his tongue against mine. He groans, and I can feel him hardening in his pants.

Our chests heave, our breaths growing labored. When he slips his cold fingers beneath my sweater, the contrast to my heated skin causes my body to tremble.

I trace my hand over the stubble lining his jaw. When he pulls back, a hint of desire is glazing over his eyes, mixed with something else. We haven't spoken those three words to each other since the night I stayed at his house. They are on the tip of my tongue now. I want so badly to say it and hear him return those feelings.

He must've sensed my hesitation. Our foreheads rest against each other's, and I tilt my head back, our labored breaths filtering against our wet skin.

"Do you know how much you mean to me, Haelynn?"

I soak in every word he says, focusing on the crack in his voice and the sensations his touch creates as he traces his fingers along my stomach.

"Yes," I breathe out.

"Do you trust me when I tell you I'll never hurt you?"

"I do."

"I love you," he whispers.

Warmth from his words spread through my body and tears prick my eyes. I grip his face in my hands and kiss him. This time, with all the passion in me, wanting him to feel how much I love him, too.

When I pull back, I breathe out the words I've been holding on to until the right moment.

"I love you too."

I roll over, moving my leg over his lap to straddle him. I wrap my arms and legs around him, holding him against me. He runs his hands along my hips, tracing the edge of my sweater before gliding them over my skin. The move sends a shiver through my body.

"I've been dreaming of you and everything about this night long before I ever even knew you. I don't know what I ever did to deserve you, but I don't want to ever lose you again."

Tears fill the brim of my eyes. I release a shuddered breath, blinking through the tears, and continue, "You've promised me over and over you'd always be here for me. You've been patient. I promise you I'm done fighting it; I'm done running. I love you, and there's nowhere else I want to be than here with you."

"You were worth it every step of the way."

I sigh. The tears that were once threatening to fall now stream down my face. I smile when Corbin brushes his thumbs under my eyes, wiping them away.

"One day soon, I'm going to get down on one knee and ask you to marry me. I'll love you until I take my last breath."

I grip his face and crash my lips against his.

When our lips break apart, he whispers against mine, "I'll never stop fighting for you, for us."

epilogue

HAELYNN
six months later

The past few months have flown by like a whirlwind. Most days, I wake up and ask myself if I'm living a dream.

I don't remember a time in my life when I was ever this happy. Even on the bad days, Corbin is next to me, reminding me we're in it together.

The judge signed off on my divorce a few days before Christmas. I never went into marriage with the thought of it ending in divorce, but the judge agreed after hearing the charges against Atlas, and he awarded me full custody of Huxton.

His trial is set for this summer, and if he's convicted, he could spend up to ten years in prison. One day, I'll be faced with the reality of him walking free, but until then, I refuse to let him continue to run my life or let me live in fear.

Life with Corbin only seems to get better with every day that passes.

We recently agreed we were ready to take our relationship a step further. When my lease was up at the end of this summer, Huxton and I would move in with him on the farm. Until then, we stayed busy on the weekend working on home renovation projects, using the time to get everything done before moving in.

The spring weather in Iowa is beautiful, with fields of flowers in full bloom and clear blue skies overhead. Madelyn gifted us with a photo session for Christmas. I wanted pictures of the three of us hung up on our walls.

"Oh, Huxie, you look so handsome." I cup my hand over my mouth when he comes running toward me. He's dressed in a light-blue polo and denim jeans, with a pair of boots matching Corbin's. He stuck his hand in his pocket, mimicking Corbin. He flashes me a wink and wiggles his brows.

"Oh my goodness, who taught you that?"

"Corbin." He grins, snapping his fingers and shooting me a finger gun.

Madelyn, who's holding her camera around her neck, slaps her hand over her mouth, attempting to contain her laughter.

"Oh Lord, help me. I'm in trouble with the two of them."

Madelyn chuckles. Corbin pushes the door open, stepping out onto the deck, and jogs down the stairs. He's wearing a pair of denim jeans, snug in all the right places, and a navy polo.

Something about the sight of Corbin in jeans and boots made it difficult to breathe. I'm reminded how much trouble I'm truly in when he notices me staring.

"You keep looking at me like that, and this photo session is about to be cut short."

My gaze darts over to him before bouncing to Madelyn's, who pursues her lips, pretending she didn't hear him. She nods her head, letting me know she had.

Corbin shrugs. "We can call it baby makin' practice."

"Baby making?" Huxton asks, squinting his eyes at Corbin in confusion.

"All right, time for pictures." I cut off the conversation before it goes any further. "Madelyn, do you have an idea of where you want us?"

We follow Madelyn toward the back of the property. I swear, the longer we've been in a relationship, the more he continues to come out of his shell.

When he's sure Huxton and Madelyn aren't looking, he reaches his hand over and grips my ass.

"Ahem, what do you think you're doing?"

"Appreciating your ass in these pants. Am I not allowed to return the favor?"

When his fingers travel lower, I clear my throat and shoo his hand away before glaring at him, warning him to behave.

He presses his lips together, smothering a laugh. He raises his hand in the air in mock surrender. He may behave now, but I know better than to think he won't try again at some point.

Madelyn runs through her ideas for pictures. She snaps a few toward the back of the property, overlooking the field lining the trees. We move back near the barn, taking a few there, too.

After about twenty minutes, Huxton gets antsy and asks if he can get back to riding his bike. He loves it out here, where he has all the space a boy needs to roam and play.

"Just a few more pictures left, buddy." Madelyn urges him to stand beside Corbin before stepping back to snap a few more.

"Haelynn," Corbin says, dropping his hand from my waist.

I peer over, expecting him to say something, when he reaches for my hand and kneels on the ground in front of me.

It takes me a second before my mind lands on what's happening. I faintly hear the sound of Madelyn snapping pictures in the background as my hand flies to my mouth.

"Corbin?"

He smiles and pulls the ring box from his pocket, opening it for me. The look of love on his face causes my breath to get caught in my throat.

I've never loved anyone the way I love him. I'm almost scared if I blink, this moment will be over, or I'll wake up to find it was all a dream.

He leans forward to kiss the back of my hand before pulling back to adjust his shoulders once again. When he goes to speak, the sound of his voice cracking causes any nerves I was feeling to melt away.

"I thought I knew what love was before I met you, but I knew from the first time I saw you, the very first kiss, my life would never be the same. You've changed me. You and Huxton have brought a happiness into my life I never knew existed. I promise to spend the rest of my life making you both as happy as you make me."

Tears flow freely down my face. I lean forward and press a kiss against his lips. When I stand, I brush my finger over his lips, wiping my lipstick off his mouth.

He rubs his lips together, lapping his tongue over them as if savoring it. The sight of him has me shaking my head, giggling.

"Let me finish, woman, then you can love on me all you want." He grins, flashing me a wink.

I smirk as he pops open the box, and my mouth drops.

"Marry me."

The sound of those two words sucks the breath out of me.

"Corbin."

"Spend forever with me. Make me the happiest man in this world. Please."

Before he has a chance to ask me again, I mutter, "Yes," before crashing my mouth back on his.

Yes. A hundred times. Every day. Without fail.

Yes.

Thank you so much for reading Where You Belong!

Still want more Corbin and Haelynn? Don't worry, I'm not done with these two yet.

Turn the page to find out how you can read their bonus epilogue. Don't miss a sneak peek at Madelyn's parents love story in Torn, a brother's best friend, small town romance.

I hope you enjoy!

BONUS SCENE

Dear Reader,

I hope you enjoyed Corbin and Haelynn story as much as I loved writing it.

I couldn't get enough of their love and wanted to give you a glimpse into their lives, so I wrote you a heartfelt bonus epilogue exclusively for you. All you have to do is visit the link below or scan the QR code with your phone, sign up for my newsletter, and you'll get access.

www.authorbrookeobrien.com/bonus

If you want to stay up to date with my sales and new releases, you can follow me on Bookbub at: www.bookbu b.com/profile/brooke-o-brien

Brooke

Torn

A TATTERED HEART DUET #1

USA TODAY BESTSELLING AUTHOR

BROOKE O'BRIEN

Prologue

MAVERICK

It was never my intention to fall in love with my best friend's sister. I was thirteen when I moved down the street from Dean Blake. He had come into my life at a time I struggled to cope with the world around me. Our friendship came without any pressures, it was easy. He didn't ask questions, but I think he knew what would happen if he did.

I closed off the door to my heart a long time ago. I didn't want to feel. The pain that comes with letting the emotions in is more than I could ever bear. Even through it all, I still remember the way I felt when I met his twin sister, Ryan. It was like a jolt to my heart, forcing it to beat out of rhythm.

Ryan was all legs, chocolate brown hair flowing in the breeze covered by her backward snapback. The first thing I noticed was the intricate detail of the designs covering her skin, like vines wrapping around her arm.

If the sweet and innocent look on her face was any indication, she was too young to have tattoos of her own. I was drawn to the outward shell she presented to the world because I recognized it for what it was. A distraction from all the parts you want to keep buried deep. She was like a mirage of walking contradictions, which I knew to be true the moment she opened her smart mouth.

The passion she withheld under the surface was like a beacon of light shining in the dark night. Her fiery personality was the first thing to trigger a spark in the hollows of my heart.

All these years I've spent keeping my distance from her, out of fear of facing my feelings and the consequences that could follow. The hard part is, I know she feels the connection between us, too. The pull that keeps us tethered to each other, despite never allowing her to get close enough.

She's turning eighteen in two days and the resistance I've been struggling to keep hold of is starting to wear thin. Nothing good can come from going down this path because no matter how much my heart aches for her, it's inevitable I'll leave her heart torn in two.

Chapter One

RYAN

"Roll the window down, it smells like sex in here!" I shout, waving my hand in front of my face. Sticking my head outside, I take a deep breath and turn my head toward my best friend with a shit eating grin on my face.

"Says the virgin," she mutters, rolling her eyes as she turns up the music to drown out any smart-ass reply I could fire back. I know she can hear me as I tell her to fuck off, which prompts her to wave her middle finger in the air at me while keeping her eyes on the road.

Papa Roach blares through the speakers, as I slide back into my seat adjusting my hat as I do. I can feel the energy from the music run through my body as I nod my head to the lyrics.

Nadia is my best friend, my A1 since day one. There's not much I wouldn't do for her and I knew it to be true from the day we first met.

We were in eighth grade, riding the bus to school, when Kara Parker thought it would be fucking funny to pick shit out of the garbage and throw it at me from where she sat in the back. She only messed with me on the days my twin brother, Dean, would opt to walk to school with his friends.

She knew better than to pull that shit around Dean.

Nadia had been sitting in the seat across from me. It was the first day we had ever talked to each other. After watching a pop bottle cap whiz past our heads, she turned toward me with her face hard as stone as she said, "You ready to put this bitch down?"

My response mirrored the same devilish grin she flashed me. She's been my ride or die ever since.

"Did you talk to your mom about staying over at my place tomorrow?" she asks, shouting over the music. Nadia's parents take on the role of parenting from a distance. They leave her money on the counter and make sure there's always food in the cabinets. Otherwise, they're hardly home, which makes it the perfect place to crash when we plan to hit up a party or two on the weekends.

"She hasn't responded to my text message yet," I mutter, clicking the button on the side of my phone to check for a response. "I'm going to call her and see." Leaning over, I turn down the radio as I click the call button.

"Big Papa's Pizzeria."

My brother's immature greeting has me rolling my eyes so hard I'm surprised they didn't pop out of my head and roll across the floor. The worst part is the annoying laugh that follows finding his lame joke funny.

"Put Mom on the phone," I snap, cutting off his obnoxious laughter, running my fingers over the frayed hole in my jeans.

"What's in it for me?"

"Staying alive. Now quit being a prick, dick licker, and put her on the phone."

"You wanna talk to your mom with that dirty mouth?" Dean laughs. I can hear the light chuckling in the background, and if I had to guess, Maverick is there with him.

Figures.

"Seriously, D. I don't have all night. If I don't talk to her now, I'm going to be home late."

"You better hope that's not the case. After the last time, you know you're going to end up grounded. Happy Birthday to you."

I can picture his smug face as he sings the last part to me and I seriously want to junk punch him.

"Alright, Dad. Noted. Now put her on the fucking phone."

I can hear the light rustling on the other end before my mom's overly chipper voice filters through the phone.

"Yes, Ryan," she says with a sigh.

"Hi, Mom," I reply, my tone extra sweet which has Nadia laughing. "Is it cool if I crash at Nadia's this weekend?"

"Not tonight, Ryan," she replies curtly. "You can tomorrow since it's your birthday, but it's not necessary to stay over two nights in a row."

"Can I stay out a little later tonight then instead? It's a Friday night and we were going to meet up with some friends."

"You've been late once already this month, even after I extended your curfew. You have until ten o'clock to be home, Ryan. By the looks of it, that gives you seventeen minutes. I'll see you soon."

Nadia glances down at the clock as the line disconnects.

"Ry, we're not going to make it in time," she says, voicing my thoughts. I don't say anything because she's right. My house is at least twenty-five minutes away on a good day.

"Shit," I groan, running my hand over my face.

Nadia does her best to get me home in time, but when we hit a train on Rockford Drive, I know it's no use.

"Look on the bright side," Nadia says, peering over at me out of the corner of her eye. "If Dean is home, that likely means Maverick is crashing at your house tonight."

Maverick is one of my brother's best friends, which is both a blessing and a curse. He and Dean never go any-where without the other. Dean is the annoying, obnoxious jock who likes to have all the attention on him. Maverick, on the other hand, is the complete opposite and sometimes I wonder what prompted their friendship.

Don't get me wrong, Dean's my twin brother, and he's a great guy. I don't know what they have in common besides skateboarding. Whatever it is, they are nearly inseparable. Maverick usually ends up staying over at our house, which I appreciate because it means I get to see him more.

"Like that matters. He acts as if I'm not there. I swear you'd think he hated me or something."

"I don't think that's true." Nadia laughs, shaking her head. "I think he's very much aware you're there. He just knows Dean would lose his shit if he knew he saw you as anything but his sister."

Which brings me to why it's a curse. Any chance of Maverick seeing me as more than his best friend's sister goes out the window. I know he would never do anything to put their friendship in jeopardy.

I can keep a secret and what Dean doesn't know won't hurt him.

Nadia whips the car into the driveway, pulling in behind Dean's beat-up Ford truck. The thing has seen better days, but he refuses to replace it.

"Text me when you can and let me know the damage," she mutters, clearly concerned our plans for tomorrow could be ruined.

I push the door of the car open and lean the seat forward, pulling out my skateboard from the backseat. I sling my backpack over my shoulder and readjust my hat on my head.

"Wish me luck," I groan, as I move the seat back in place.

We say our goodbyes as I head toward the front of my house.

My mom is in the kitchen loading the dishwasher when I enter the house. She doesn't bother to look at me, which I know can't be good. Kicking my shoes off near the door, I prop my board against the wall.

I spot Dean and Maverick lounging in the living room. Dean has his leg draped across the coffee table and a grin on his face, knowing what's about to come. Maverick grimaces and I know this can't be good.

"Welcome home," my mother says, the force of the dishwasher closing draws my attention away from him.

"Ryan, this is the second time you've been late this month. Before you even try to argue, I want to point out your birthday is in less than two hours, and I know you have plans with Nadia."

Dropping my bag down on the bench near the door, I slide the hat off my head and toss it on top before facing my mom.

"I'm sorry," I sigh, knowing nothing good will come from me saying anything more. "I'm going to bed."

I walk through the kitchen and into the living room. The urge to junk punch Dean has returned when I see the arrogant smirk on his face.

"Keep it up, fucker," I mutter under my breath, careful to not let my mom overhear us as I flash him the finger.

"What's that?" he retorts, turning his head to peer over the back of the couch.

Spinning around, I find both of their eyes on me. Seeing that my mom has since made her way out of the kitchen, likely retreating to our parents' bedroom, I don't hold back.

"I said keep it up, fucker. I should be the one laughin' at you, sitting at home like a bum on a Friday night," I snap, sounding bored as I lean against the wall.

There are about seven minutes separating the two of us. My parents were expecting to bring home two baby boys when I was born. What they didn't expect was for the second child to be born a girl. My name is evidence of that.

Dean turns around, facing the TV and lets out an annoyed grunt, "Fuck off, Ry."

My eyes bounce from Dean to Maverick and I'm surprised when I find Maverick's are already on me. They shine bright with amusement, as he bites his lower lip in an attempt to hide the grin lining his mouth. Crossing his arms over his chest, he runs his hand over his jaw as he glances over to make sure Dean isn't paying attention.

The thick muscles are tanned from all his days outside without his T-shirt on. His dark-brown hair is longer on top. The wayward strands give the appearance like he has ran his fingers through them one too many times.

The sleeves of my white T-shirt are cut off, giving it more of a muscle-shirt look. You can see my black sports bra from the side and a hint of my sun-kissed skin underneath.

My heart starts to pound as I relish the thought of him struggling to take his eyes off me. Taking two steps backward, I keep my eyes trained on him. I think back to my conversation with Nadia in the car when she said it's Dean that's holding him back.

The bold side of me wants to test her theory and see if it's true.

Standing outside my bedroom door, I keep my eyes focused on Maverick as I grab the hem of my shirt and pull the cotton material over my head. I roll my shirt into a ball before tossing it in the direction of my dirty clothes but not bothering to check if it made it.

I watch as Maverick's jaw clenches as his eyes travel over the length of my body, resting longer on my chest than necessary before finally bringing his eyes up to meet mine. He leans forward, pressing his elbows to his knees. Even then, he doesn't take his eyes off me.

"D, I'm gonna use your bathroom quick and head out. I should've been home a little while ago."

I can hear Dean mumble out a response, but I have no idea what he says. I'm too lost in the look on Maverick's face to pay much attention to what is going on around me.

Bracing his palms on his knees, Maverick moves to stand. He's so tall, standing over six feet. He's athletic, but whereas my brother is stockier from his time in football, Maverick is lean.

I can hear my heart pounding in my ears as he stalks toward me with a slight tic in his jaw. The closer he gets to me, the more my body comes alive with his presence.

"A little bold of you. Wouldn't you say, Rebel?"

It isn't the first time I've heard him use the nickname, but the tone in his voice is deeper. I can feel the words roll through me, crashing over me like waves as he stands close leaving only an inch between us.

I'm not able to think properly as I stare up at his gray eyes. They're so dark, it's almost like a storm is brewing in their depths.

Raising his hand up, he runs his knuckle along the soft skin of my shoulder as I force a step away from him. I need to gain some semblance of sanity, but the move causes his lip to curl in a small grin.

"You have nothing to say now? I didn't think that was possible." His quiet chuckle does crazy things to my heart.

"Aren't you supposed to be leaving now?" I retort, hating how he can look so unaffected knowing the way he's making me feel.

"Yeah, I am. Are you sure it's what you want though?"

He presses the palm of his hand against my hip as he moves to step closer in the narrow hallway. I'm standing so close to the wall, I know there's plenty of room for him to pass by.

His thumb lightly traces my exposed skin, as he takes a step around me. His body is pressed against mine, bringing us closer than we've ever been.

The move forces the air out of my chest and I know he can feel my body tremble beneath his touch.

"I didn't think so," he whispers against the shell of my ear.

As soon as he passes by me and the bathroom, he glances back at me. His eyes travel down to where my chest heaves with every struggled breath before looking back up at me. Flashing me a wink, he turns and walks down the hallway and out the front door without another word.

Holy shit.

Do you want more Maverick and Ryan?
Check out Torn today!

BOOKS BY BROOKE

A Rebels Havoc Series

Brix
Sins of a Rebel
Tysin
Trey
Madden

Men of Blaze

Personal Foul
Reckless Rebound (Cocky Hero Club)

Tattered Heart Duet

Torn
Tattered

A Heart's Compass Series

Where I Found You
Lost Before You
Until I Found You
Now That I Found You
Where You Belong

Standalones (In order of publication)

Wild Irish

Learn more and purchase your copy at:
www.authorbrookeobrien.com/booksbybrooke

ACKNOWLEDGMENTS

To my boys – I love you more than the universe. Thank you for thinking I'm cool and for being proud of mama for writing books, even though it makes me cringe to think about you telling your teachers. We'll just pretend that doesn't happen.

To my AMAZING beta readers – Thorunn, Kristen, Summer, April, Candyce, and Donna. Thank you for reading Corbin and Haelynn's story before anyone else, for your honest feedback, and for helping me make their story better. I'm so grateful to you! <3

Jenny Sims, Amy Briggs, and Rox LeBlanc – Thank you for your hard work on this project. You both have been so wonderful to work with and learn from. I wouldn't want to do this without you on my team!

To the fantastic bloggers and my Rebel Hype Team, thank you for being a part of this one. I'm excited to hear what you think of Corbin and Haelynn. I hope you know how grateful I am for every one of you.

My Rebels Readers – I love being able to connect with all of you in my Reader Group and across social media. Thank you for your love of this series. It's changed my life and I'm so thankful for you all!

Thorunn – We've grown close so quickly, and I can't tell you how much it's meant having your friendship and support over the past year. Thank you for always being a listening ear and sharing your opinion. It means a lot to me!

April – Thank you so much for being you. We've grown so close over the past few years and I'm thankful to have you and your sense of humor in my life. There's never a dull moment when we're together. I love having you as my book friend and my real friend.

Kristen – Thank you for always being honest with me, no matter what. I can always count on you to keep it real and raw with me. Even when I think every word I've written is shit, you're there to bring me back to earth. I love you!

Kate Jessop and Lyssa Cole – Thank you for your friendship and support, for checking in with me, and letting me bounce ideas off you. Your friendship and support mean the world to me.

ABOUT BROOKE

USA Today Bestselling author Brooke O'Brien writes steamy and swoon-worthy new adult romances. She's best known for her sports and rock star romances.

Brooke believes a love worth having is worth fighting for, and she brings this into her stories where her characters risk it all for love.

When she isn't writing or falling in love with a new book boyfriend, you can find her spending time with her family, cheering on her favorite sports teams, listening to ASMR, or binge-watching the latest true crime documentary. She loves rockin' a comfy hoodie with leggings and believes the best days include a good nap.

Brooke loves connecting with readers and hopes you'll join her on her social pages or reader group to stay in touch. To follow Brooke and join her newsletter, visit authorbro okeobrien.com/follow.

COPYRIGHT

Where You Belong: A Heart's Compass Novel
Copyright © 2023 by Brooke O'Brien with Tattered Ink Publishing
All Rights Reserved

No part of this book may be reproduced or transmitted in any form or by any means, electronic or mechanical, including photocopying, recording, or by any information storage and retrieval system without written permissions of the author, except for the use of brief quotations in a review.

This is a work of fiction. Names, characters, places and incidents either are the product of the author's imagination or are used fictitiously. Any resemblance to persons, living or dead, business establishments, events, or locales is entirely coincidental. The author acknowledges the trademarked status and trademark owners of various products referenced in this work of fiction, which has been used without permission. The publication/use of these trademarks is not authorized, associated with or sponsored by the trademark owners.

For information on subsidiary rights, please contact Tattered Ink Publishing at .

Edited by Amy Briggs with Briggs Consulting LLC
Proofread by Rox LeBlanc with Rox's Reads and Jenny Sims
with Editing for Indies
Najla Qamber with Najla Qamber Designs
  Version: BMO08042023